Kissing Lots of Frogs

A Long Journey to Love

Rosemary Strouse Clifton

PublishAmerica
Baltimore

First printing

At the specific preference of the author, PublishAmerica allowed this work to remain exactly as the author intended, verbatim, without editorial input.

ISBN: 1-4241-1027-0
PUBLISHED BY PUBLISHAMERICA, LLLP
www.publishamerica.com
Baltimore

Printed in the United States of America

Dedicated to my dear husband, Ron, my prince.

Jean —
I've enjoyed
meeting you —
very much!
Gail [illegible]

*Thank you, Dear God, for my memories,
for my imagination, and for the ability to
tell which is which.*

Foreword

Carrie realized she had never had a happy love affair. Oh, there had been lots of men. Too many men. Too many men with too many problems. Or were the problems hers? Why couldn't she find someone? She felt she was attractive, bright, and pleasant. She even double-checked her assessment with friends. What's the problem? She was tired of the core of loneliness that haunted her life. She felt she was living a Country-Western song. In fact, when she writes her life story, she tells herself she's going to give each chapter the name of a Country-Western song—there's definitely a song to cover every kind of loneliness and pain she's felt.

The Last Word in Lonesome is Me

"I've dated a lot and, in this world of senior dating, not all flakes are dandruff, if you know what I mean," Carrie said. Greg and Carrie had spent most of their first date discussing the joys and pitfalls of the single scene in Florida, especially in Sun View, the over fifty-five retirement community in which they both lived.

"You're probably right, although I haven't met too many flakes. I hope you don't think I'm one," Greg said.

"Not at all. You seem like a nice, well-adjusted guy. In fact, I enjoyed this evening very much," Carrie said as they arrived in front of her home. "I would invite you in, but I have an early morning meeting."

Carrie is a tireless volunteer who attends lots of meetings. She finds being active in clubs a good way to get to know others. Folks are always asking her how she spends so much time working for many organizations. What they don't know is that's all she has. Her second husband died a few years ago. She has no money to travel so she fills her time helping others.

"Why don't we do it again?" Greg was a tall, good-looking guy with a confident air. He had no doubt the evening had gone well and Carrie would go out with him again.

"I don't know, Greg, whether I want to."

"What? I thought you had a good time?" Greg knew he looked good. The ladies loved his head full of white hair. He had taken Carrie into a neighboring town to the newly-renovated Longhorn Restaurant. He made sure he took her somewhere nice, not one of the few mediocre restaurants in Sun View. He couldn't figure out her answer. Had he forgotten his deodorant? He thought of the old joke that he had worn his Right Guard but forgot his Left Guard.

"Oh, I definitely had a nice time, but I'm looking for something special in a relationship."

"Well, for pity sakes, how can you tell anything about how a relationship will develop in one date?" Greg was thinking that Carrie might be a mental case. *The lights are on but no one's home. What was there not to like? And now she wants a special relationship. Please.*

"I think you're a wonderful guy. You're handsome, nice, smart, and a community leader."

Maybe she's not so mental after all. "So what's missing? Isn't there any chemistry?" *Maybe I should have hit on her right away.*

"Yes, I'm also very attracted to you." Carrie really didn't feel like having this little talk now, but decided she might as well go ahead, as he was so inquisitive. "I need to fill you in on a little of my background."

"I'm listening." *This oughta be good.*

"I've been married twice. My first husband left me, and my second husband died. In both cases, I took care of them—the first one financially and constant care-giving for the second. I'm tired of supporting men. I want a man who will take care of me."

"Are you saying that you want a sugar daddy?" *Okay, now I understand. She wants someone to support her. Pay her bills. She doesn't care about anything else. This is every woman's dream—to have four animals—a mink on her back, a jaguar in the garage, a tiger in bed, and a jackass to pay for all of it.* Greg's sarcastic sense of humor worked even when he was apparently being dumped.

"No, not exactly. I have enough money to pay my bills—my home, clothes, car, so forth. What I can't afford are all the little extras that make life fun. My first husband went through a lot of my money, and the medical bills for my second husband left me with very little in the bank."

"Well, I can certainly afford to take you out to dinner, if that's all you're worried about." Greg kept trying, although he was beginning to see the handwriting on the wall. In fact, it was looking like very large, ugly graffiti. It reminded Greg of something he had read on the Internet recently—there are a number of mechanical devices that increase sexual arousal in women. Chief among these is the Mercedes-Benz SL 500.

"No, I want more than dinner. I want to be taken on at least two vacations a year. I do want to go out to dinner a lot, but I want my way paid everywhere we go—dances, parties, concerts, cruises, and so forth. You, if anyone, certainly know how much there is to do in this town, but I really can't afford to do any of it.

Carrie continued, "While I'm wishing, I'll add that I want a substantial birthday and Christmas gift of my choosing each year. An occasional piece of jewelry would be nice. In other words, I want to be treated like a queen."

"Interesting! You certainly have it all figured out. Do you give anything in return?" *Get me out of here. I gotta stick around long enough to see where this goes, though.*

"I would be a very loving and faithful companion."

That's big of you, lady. "Is marriage in this plan?"

"Nope! No marriage. No living together. In fact, I will only be loving and faithful while my guy is alive and well. If he gets sick, I will visit him and be his friend but not take care of him."

"You know, you might be the one who gets sick and needs someone." *Does she think she's immune to illness?*

"Nope. I have made provisions for that eventuality. I would not stick a man with my care."

"Well, these requirements certainly put a different light on everything. Don't I get any points for being handsome, nice—and all the other things you said?"

"Yes, you do, but my top priority is finding a man that will put some fun in my life. All I can afford to do is sit at home. I don't have the money to take advantage of all of this town's activities, cheap as they are."

Carrie continued, "So I want someone who will help me have a good time and who will be a wonderful companion. And oh, by the way, I would like to be physically attracted to him, too. I think I can find a man with it all. Are you interested, now that you've heard my requirements?"

"I don't know. I'll have to think about it. It almost sounds too much like a business proposition or worse." *Good luck, lady. You'll never find anyone who'll go for this crazy arrangement. Especially not me.*

"Let me know. I'll be out there looking," Carrie said as she exited the car quickly and headed for her front door.

Inside her beautifully decorated living room, Carrie collapsed on her leather sofa and laughed at herself. Here she was trying to find a man with money. Actually a man who would truly love her would be enough.

After staring into space for a few minutes, she remembered her music. It was the one thing that gave her solace. She walked to her CD collection and selected five Country music discs. After nestling into the sofa again, she listened to the music. Oh, how she loved Country music. She was not raised in the country. She did not even particularly admire the country life style. No farms or ranches for her.

What she related to was the loneliness of the songs. Carrie wiped away a tear. Yes, she related to loneliness—she had been lonely most of her life. Not alone, but lonely. There had been many men pass through her life, most of whom had told her they loved her. Another tear rolled down her cheek as she remembered, just as in the songs, unrequited love, cheating men, and hard-hearted lovers. The list of love affairs that didn't work out could go on and on. In fact, she felt she had an experience for every song out there. If she ever wrote a book about her life, she would pick a different, appropriate Country music song to be the title of each chapter.

Carrie walked to the back door where her dog was pacing to be let out. "Time to go out, Charley, and do your business. Hurry back, though. I can use some fluffy puppy love tonight."

Here Stands the Glass—Fill It to the Brim

"Stay free for lunch," was all the voicemail message said. There was no identification of the caller. Of course, Carrie knew right away who it was. She thought it was very brash of Ray even though she knew last night, when she met him, that he was a forward man. While it wasn't love at first sight with Ray, Carrie did find him very appealing.

"I'll stay free for lunch, all right," she thought to herself. "I'm always free, here at home, eating my peanut butter sandwiches."

At precisely noon the telephone rang. "I'm out front in a taxi. Come on out, and we'll go to Sarasota for lunch."

"Okay," was all Carrie could manage. "In a cab?"

"Yeah, I don't like messing with rental cars."

Well, he's either very rich or very poor. Maybe, very dumb. Carrie was muttering to herself. *Let's hope it's very rich, and then my search for Mr. Wonderful might be over before it gets started.*

Carrie slipped into a basic black pants-suit with lime-green camisole top. She hated her figure and hid out in black a lot. She particularly disliked her legs so she wore pants often. In fact, in her opinion, her boobs were her only good feature so she tried to enhance them a lot with décolleté tanks.

When Carrie got in the taxi, there was Ray with the largest bouquet of roses she had ever seen. It seemed like there must have been two hundred flowers. She knew there weren't that many, but she didn't want to seem like a hick and count them.

The roses were a sharp contrast to the cab which, while not broken down, was not one of the later models. The flowers helped a little to camouflage the stale tobacco smell. She hoped Ray was not a smoker. Soon she found out it was the cabbie as she watched him light cigarette after cigarette on their drive to Sarasota. Fortunately, there was a partition between the front and back seats.

"Wow, for me? What did I do to deserve all these roses?"

"It's what you're going to do."

"That doesn't sound too good." Carrie was getting nervous and hoped that she hadn't given him the wrong impression in the Wooden Nickel. She wasn't sleepy after bridge last night and had stopped in the tavern for a glass of wine. She knew Ray had been attracted to her but thought it was a little too soon for him to be making assumptions about their relationship.

"You're going to be the love of my life. Stick with me, babe. We'll have the time of our lives. I've been looking for a gal like you." Ray was a good-looking blonde, a little stocky, but good-looking, nonetheless. And he acted like he knew he was attractive. He said what he thought in a very forceful way. He certainly was no mealy-mouth. Carrie always fell for guys who exuded power, whether it was real or not.

Carrie nervously chatted away on the trip to Sarasota. Ray had reservations at the fanciest restaurant he could find on the water—Christopher's. It promised to be a lovely lunch. It was a gorgeous day with a temperature of about 75 degrees. The sun's reflection twinkled on the blue water they could see out the restaurant window. Of course, Ray had insisted on a table with a view.

"Would you like something to drink, perhaps some wine," Ray asked.

"Some wine would be nice. You'll join me, of course?"

"Oh, no, I never drink at lunch. Working, you know."

"Refresh my memory, please. What exactly is your work?" Carrie was curious.

"I'm in electrical and mechanical contracting."

"Would that be residential?" Carrie was anxious to know what he did that allowed him to buy lots of roses on a whim and take taxi-cabs everywhere.

"No, unfortunately, it's not quite that easy. I oversee the electrical and mechanical contracting work for all the malls that the Rouse Company builds world-wide. At any one time they have several malls in various stages of development, and I travel all the time, checking progress, particularly in the heating and air conditioning areas."

"That's interesting." Carrie wasn't quite sure what to say. *Oh, great, a technoid. Hopefully, he won't be a colossal bore.*

"Right now I'm concentrating on that big mall that's under development in Tampa. One of these days I will take you there and show you what I do."

The lunch lasted a couple of hours and then they headed back to Sun View. Actually Ray wasn't a bore at all. He was a rather exciting character. He had lots of stories about his travels and some funny ones about things that had gone awry in malls around the country. At the end of lunch, Ray said, "I want you to go to dinner with me tomorrow night. I'll pick you up at six o'clock. Okay?"

***

"Judy, this may be my dream man. He's definitely a take-charge type, which I like. He's attractive, and he's buying me things already! Here I come, world, out of my humdrum existence!"

"Be careful, Carrie. You should check this guy out. At least call the home office in Maryland and see if he really does work there." Judy, Carrie's best friend, was always full of practical advice. Judy was a widow, having lost her husband of many years to lung cancer. It had only been a couple of years since his death so Judy was still adjusting to being alone.

"I beat you to the punch. I've already checked up on him. His secretary said that he wasn't in, that he was on the road this week so at least they've heard of him."

***

"You're one gorgeous lady. I love a woman that really knows how to dress." Carrie was glad she had picked her black two-piece outfit that had lots of rhinestones scattered on it. Her flared sleeves were studded with them from the elbow down to the wrist and the flared pants legs were studded from the knee down to her ankles. Of course, the top was low-cut, not much, but enough to be sexy.

"Thank you, sir. You look very nice yourself." Ray had on a nicely-tailored business suit, as he always did. "Where are we headed tonight?" Carrie asked.

"We're going to the Tampa Marriott Waterside Hotel for dinner. That's where I'm staying, and they have a wonderful chef. The terrace is delightful for dining."

***

"How about some wine this evening? I'll join you in a little drinkie-poo."

Drinkie-poo? That sounds so retarded. I guess Ray's just being silly.

"Would the gentleman like to select the wine that you two will be enjoying?" the waiter asked.

"I'll let you recommend for the lady. I'll have a double martini," Ray said.

The evening progressed with a lot of good conversation. Ray was humorous and had lots of stories. His tales got longer and funnier as he downed six or seven double martinis. Drinkie-poo didn't sound exactly right to Carrie for the type of drink and quantity he was slugging down. She hoped he didn't use silly talk too much. She knew he was just trying to be cute, but it definitely took away from her image of him.

At one point Ray asked, "What are you doing in Sun View? I know it's an over-55 community, and you certainly aren't that old. How old are you anyway?"

"Well, you're lucky I'm one of those ladies who doesn't mind revealing her age. I'm 54."

"So how'd you get in?"

"My late husband was quite a bit older. He definitely was qualified to live in Sun View."

Being satisfied with that answer, Ray changed the subject. "Let's go up to my room," he said at about nine o'clock.

"Oh, no, I don't think I should do that."

"Well, then, the cab will take you home. The driver has my charge code so you don't need to pay him anything. No tip, no nothing. You do know that eventually I'll want you to stay overnight with me in my room? Get ready for it."

***

"I don't know what to think, Judy. He was fun and basically a gentleman although he wanted me to follow him to his room."

"My gosh, he hasn't even kissed you yet, and already he wants your bod!"

"No, he did give me a kiss, sweet but a little boozy. And guess what else he gave me—a beautiful gold bracelet. He said he noticed that I liked bangle bracelets. See how thoughtful he is?" Carrie held out her arm and showed Judy the shiny twisted rope bangle.

***

Carrie continued to see Ray whenever he was in town. For many months the routine was the same—dinner at some elegant restaurant, lots of drinks, a trip to Ray's room, an expensive gift, and a lonely ride home in the cab.

"I have a surprise for you tonight."

"What's that?" Carrie was always being surprised by Ray so his announcement was not astonishing.

"We're going to New York City for three weeks."

"Who is *we*?"

"You and me, babe. We're going to have a blast—theatre, dancing, dining. You name it. We'll do it. I'll be there to work, but I don't really have much to do for the company this trip."

***

"Are you going?" Judy wanted to know.

"Yes, I am. I can't pass up an opportunity like this, although I don't know whether his drinking will get to me when I'm with him 24 hours a day."

"He's an alcoholic," Judy announced.

"He is not!"

"Carrie, he's an alcoholic."

"He can't be. He has a responsible job and never drinks during the day."

"Alcoholics come in all sizes and shapes. From what you've told me, Ray's pattern is to start drinking at five o'clock in the afternoon and drink all evening. He's basically comatose by nine o'clock. Am I right?" Judy was wound up now.

"You're right, but he's a nice drunk, and I'm going to New York with him. That's final."

***

"Let's go to the Rainbow Room tonight, babe, okay?"

"I'd love it." The days and nights were filled with wonderful Big Apple activities. There were lunch at Garden on the Green and a carriage ride in Central Park. Somehow Ray managed to get tickets to all the popular shows on Broadway. If it wasn't a show they were attending, then it was an evening in one of the many comedy clubs.

At one small club where Ray and Carrie were sitting ringside, Joan Rivers was making one of her rare appearances. She doesn't do much standup comedy anymore, but somehow Ray found out she was performing that night. She was into her routine. The crowd was going wild at her jokes. Ray was drinking heavily plus it was way past his usual self-imposed nine o'clock curfew.

"I just got back from a short trip to Baltimore. That's the town that gave us Wallis Warfield Simpson." Joan was setting up a joke.

"Hey, leave Mrs. Simpson alone." Carrie couldn't believe Ray had shouted out for all to hear.

"Sir, this is just a joke." Joan was trying to alleviate the situation.

In a very drunken, slurred speech, Ray said, "I'm from Baltimore, and we don't make fun of Wallis Warfield Simpson."

"Sir, it's a joke. I'm sure she was a very nice lady."

"She was from Baltimore, you know?"

"Yes, sir, I know. That's how I started my joke, if you recall."

Carrie felt like crawling under the table and out the door. Finally Ray shut up.

In the morning everything was fine again. Carrie knew she had several hours of Ray's civilized behavior before the cocktail hour. She looked forward to the days and dreaded the evenings. Carrie loved all the wonderful restaurants in which they dined. There are thousands of restaurants in the city, and Carrie felt like she had been to most of them. However, she hated trying to carry on a conversation with a drunk.

The last straw was one of their final evenings in New York City. They attended a late concert at the Waldorf Astoria featuring Harry Connick, Jr. Every time there was silence in the performance, Ray would shake his glass. He thought it was cute.

"Ray, please stop tinkling your ice," Carrie said in a hushed tone.

"I'll tinkle if I want to," Ray announced at the top of his lungs. At that, Carrie was so outraged she upset a water glass, and it was dripping down her skirt but she was too paralyzed to move or right the glass.

"I'm leaving," Carrie said. Falling over everyone, Ray followed Carrie out of the room.

In the hotel room Ray tried to apologize to Carrie by roughly grabbing her and pulling her to him. In his drunken state he didn't know his own strength. However, Carrie somehow found the strength to shove him away.

"You're trying to push me out the 18th floor window," Ray accused.

That was it! Carrie packed up her belongings while Ray was passed out on the bed. She left without saying goodbye.

***

"Okay, don't say 'I told you so.'" Carrie was relating the story to Judy. "It was the definitive trip to NYC, okay? I don't think there was anything in that city that I didn't see. So he was a drunk. So, okay. I got a lot of nice jewelry out of the relationship. That's more than a lot of women end up with."

"Are you going to see him again?"

"Never! I'll miss the jewelry but not the conversations with a drunk, if you want to call them conversations. And I sure won't miss the sex. How would you like to be ridden for hours on end?"

Judy said, "A lot of women dream of that."

"Believe me, it's a nightmare. Oh, maybe it's fun for the first hour while I climaxed a couple of times. However, after that it's agony waiting for him to come. He never could when he was drunk. It always ended up with my begging him to get off of me."

"So it's over?"

It's over! And furthermore, I will never, ever date a drunk again. Not for trips. Not for jewelry. Not for anything. It was a very sobering experience. It's back to staying home and peanut butter sandwiches for me."

Breaking in a Brand New Broken Heart

"Mark can't afford you." Judy ventured her opinion as usual. "You want a man who can spend money on you. I don't think Mark's the one."

"Well, so far, so good. He always takes me somewhere really nice, and I received a lovely birthday gift from him." Mark was a guy Carrie met while dating Ray. When Carrie left Ray after a year-long ordeal with his drunkenness, Mark wasted no time asking Carrie out. Carrie was attracted to Mark, she surmised, because he was the exact opposite of Ray. She had gotten burned out on Ray's brashness. You couldn't push Mark around, but he definitely wasn't brash.

"Carrie, Mark's just been dumped! He has an ex-wife and two children to support."

"I know, but he's *Philadelphia Main Line*—old Pennsylvania Rail Road money."

"How old is he, anyway?"

"Fifty."

"Fifty, and he has young children?" Judy was surprised.

"This was a second marriage for him. His wife was quite a bit younger than he was."

***

"I had a huge crush on you when you were dating Ray," Mark said. "When the three of us went to dinner together, I had a hard time keeping my eyes off of you."

"I never knew. You never said anything or let on."

"That would not have been proper. Ray is my best friend from childhood, you know, but I sure was glad when you broke up."

"I'm sort of surprised that you want to date," Carrie opened the "divorce" conversation.

"It's difficult, but I need to get on with my life."

"What happened?" Carried asked.

"Sally fell in love with a tomato farmer."

"What? You're kidding!"

"No, can you believe a young socialite, who has everything, falling in love with a dirt-covered crum bum? She ran off with him and took the kids." Mark seemed embarrassed telling Carrie the situation. "Sally was the daughter of the CEO of one of the largest insurance companies in the United States. She was used to money and had been raised to enjoy the finer things of life. This tomato farmer was a liberal, rabble-rouser, who was always espousing upheaval for the downtrodden. I guess Sally fell under his spell. Supposedly, he was pretty charismatic."

***

Even though good friends, Mark and Ray were nothing alike. Mark was quiet, well-mannered, respectful, very attentive—a class act. And, he was just a light social drinker. No alcohol problems here.

Carrie and Mark's dates usually consisted of dinner in a nice restaurant and lots of conversation, often about his ex-wife or his children. The talk would continue late into the night at his home. Mark was such a nice guy that Carrie believed she was falling in love with him.

***

"Doesn't he ever talk about *your* relationship?" Judy was at it again.

"Yes, he's even started telling me that he loves me and that I'm helping him adjust. He always tells me how appreciative he is."

"I would think the talking about his ex-wife would get old, Carrie."

"I know. I know. At least both of my husbands hated their ex-wives and never talked about them. I think Mark is still in love with Sally and would take her back in a heartbeat—just a feeling I have," Carrie admitted. "But I also know that he knows it's not going to happen."

Their dates started including his children. Most of their activities revolved around the kids' interests. They adored their father but did not exclude Carrie on their weekend visitations. In fact, Carrie was growing quite fond of Mark Jr. and Lindsay. She felt like she was in love with three people. She looked forward to every weekend when the four of them would spend both days together. There were picnics, movies, and lots of pool parties. The days were for the kids, but the evenings were devoted to adult activities.

Then came the fateful weekend—the weekend when everything changed. Carrie waited for Mark's phone call. *What's wrong? He always calls me by noon on Friday.* She waited and waited. By four o'clock. she was sure something terrible had happened. Against her better judgment, Carrie called him at his work in a neighboring town.

"Mark, I'm glad I got you. What's wrong?"

"What do you mean 'what's wrong?'"

"You always call me by noon on Friday and let me know what we're all going to do this weekend."

"I'm sorry, Carrie. I should have told you last night." Mark sounded sad.

"Should have told me what?"

"I've decided that it's not good for the kids to get so attached to you."

"What? We're already attached. I love those kids."

"And they love you, but it's not right. Something could happen to our relationship and then they would be devastated. I want to break off the kids' association with you except for rare occasions. You can understand that, can't you, Carrie?"

"But you only get the kids on the weekends. Does that mean I'm not going to see you anymore on Saturday and Sunday?"

"I'm afraid it does, but we'll have plenty of other time together. We can still see each other a couple of nights each week.

Carrie accepted the conditions although she didn't like them at all. Mark continued to date Carrie, but things were never quite the same. Carrie sat home many nights and cried about their limited relationship.

New Year's Eve was coming up. Carrie was glad that there would be a new year, maybe a new start. She wondered when Mark would tell her what they were going to do for the usually festive evening. Finally she decided to ask him.

"Oh, I don't know. I'll think of something," Mark said.

The evening grew closer. Carrie was getting upset about not knowing. She did not want to sit home on New Year's Eve. She had done that for too many years. Now that she had a man in her life, she wanted to celebrate.

She knew it was wrong but she decided to manipulate him a little. She tried to sound lighthearted and like she was joking. "Mark, if you don't let me know pretty soon, I'm going to have to get another date." Mark just looked at her, somewhat in disbelief.

Two more weeks went by and still no plans for the big night from Mark. Carrie couldn't stand it any longer. "Mark, are we going to do something New Year's Eve or not? We need to make reservations."

"Well, no. When you told me you were going to get another date for the evening, I decided to find someone else to take out."

"You what?" Carrie was choking up now. "I was only kidding."

"It didn't sound like kidding to me. It sounded like a threat. I don't like threats."

"Who is she?"

"Oh, a gal in my office. Don't worry. Everything's all right between you and me. I'll call you Sunday."

Carrie hated herself for what she did. *Talk about a backfire! I should have known better. Manipulation never works except on the youngest or dumbest*. She spent a miserable evening. New Year's Eve was on a Saturday night this year. What was worse was that Mark never called on Sunday as he promised.

By Monday morning Carrie was panicking. *What the heck is going on?* By now she was about out of her mind with anger, jealousy, curiosity, and worry.

***

"You did what!" Judy was shouting at Carrie.

"I just had to find out what was going on."

"You're lucky you didn't get shot."

"I was careful. I let myself in his front door with the key he had given me."

"Go on," Judy said. Her curiosity and pure disbelief were making her impatient.

"Well, right inside the door, I knew it was over. There on the floor was a handbag, beautiful fuchsia sequined evening gown in a heap, high heels, hose, and worst of all, panties and bra. It took me a few seconds to comprehend what was going on."

"Yes, yes! What happened next?"

"I tip-toed into the master bedroom and started looking around. All of a sudden I realized that someone was in the king-size bed. The person was not moving and seemed to be sleeping. I leaned way over the bed to get a better look and almost fell in. Sure enough, the girl in the bed matched the description of Mark's New Year's Eve date. She was a redhead just like me, but she had short curly hair."

"Oh, my God. They spent the entire weekend in bed."

"You got it. Mark went to work Monday morning and left her sleeping."

"What did you do next?"

"I tip-toed back into the entryway and looked in her wallet for identification. I don't know why I did that. I knew it was over. I went home and called Mark."

"I said 'Gee, Mark, I hope I didn't mess anything up for you but I just met your new girlfriend in your bed.' I then slammed down the receiver and cried for the rest of the day."

"I'm past it all, Judy. I know this sounds like sour grapes, but he wasn't very well-endowed. Mark was only 5'7" but had a wonderful physique, lightly muscled, but with what you would call a well-proportioned, slight build. It was like everything was in miniature including his cock."

"That shouldn't matter," Judy offered.

"Obviously, you've never been screwed by a three-inch dick."

"Well, I've only been screwed, as you put it, by my late husband. Fortunately, I guess, his penis was bigger than three inches."

"I will give Mark credit, though, he made the most of what he had. He was great at foreplay."

"Forget his three-inch dick," Judy said, "I hope you learned your lessons."

"What lessons?"

"Don't ever manipulate. But more importantly, don't ever date a guy who has just been dumped. He has way too much adjusting to do for a year or two. You were a therapist to him. Once he was healed, he needed to move on. Get it?"

"Got it!"

Help Me Make It Through the Night

Who's that gorgeous creature? Carrie had been checking out the dancers when she spotted a tall, good-looking guy, dancing very stiffly around the floor. His posture was great, but he looked somewhat dazed behind his stylish, wire-rimmed glasses.

I hope he's not bombed out of his mind! I'm going to find out on the next 'ladies choice' dance.

Slowly Carrie crossed the room to where he was leaning against the wall. "Hi, I'm Carrie. Will you dance with me?"

"Well...uh...okay."

"What's your name?"

"Frank."

"You're not a big conversationalist, are you, Frank?"

"What do you mean by that?" Frank sounded a little threatened.

"I'm just kidding," Carrie apologized.

"I'm sorry," Frank said. "I'm just a little nervous. I'm here under false pretenses."

"What do you mean?"

"This is Parents Without Partners, right? Most of the folks here are looking to make a match with someone with kids. My kids are all grown and have kids of their own." Carrie had heard the organization in the neighboring town was a great place to meet middle-aged singles. She was getting tired of the older guys in Sun View.

"That's nothing, Frank. I don't even have any children."

"What?" Frank was baffled. "How'd you get in?"

"For ten years I paid child support for my first husband's son. I figure I can claim him even though I never once met the boy!"

"You mean that you paid money out of your own pocket?" Frank was curious now.

"Yes, I totally supported my first husband for ten years. It's a long story—weird but true."

Frank warmed up, and he and Carrie danced the rest of the evening. The room in the motel that Parents without Partners had rented seemed dark and dismal, but dancing with Frank made Carrie feel very romantic. She glided around the room in Frank's arms daydreaming about falling in love again. Frank broke her reverie by saying, "I would like to see you again, but I'm leaving on a trip to Virginia the first thing tomorrow morning. May I call you from there?"

***

Carrie's hand was asleep, and her ear ached. They had been talking for four hours on the telephone. To be comfortable, she had gotten in bed while she talked with Frank. In the last few days they had talked for many long hours. Carrie was getting to know Frank very well, she thought.

"There's something I need to tell you, Carrie. I'm disabled."

"You looked pretty healthy to me, Frank." Frank had good posture, didn't limp, and showed no signs of being handicapped.

"I have episodes of great fear and panic."

After a pause while Carrie thought about fear and panic as a disability, she finally asked, "Is this something you were born with?"

"No, when I worked, a giant of a man, who was a paranoid schizophrenic, decided that he didn't like the way I smiled at him, and he beat me up. I was in a coma for five days."

"You seemed to have recovered very well."

"No, not really. I have a lot of pain and a severe phobia—I don't like crowds or any other threatening situation. When I am in public, I must always sit with my back to the wall. I have a fear of being attacked again."

"I hope you sued."

"Yes, I got a very large amount of money from the contractor. They knew that the guy was a sicko, but kept him on the payroll anyway."

Frank and Carrie started to date, most of the time anyway. Several times

Frank would not call for days. Carrie would call to find out if he were okay. Often he would not answer the phone. Sometimes, though, he would answer with a very slurred voice. Carrie knew that Frank didn't drink so she just assumed that he was very tired or having a bad spell with his phobia.

***

"Can you believe it, Judy? I won two free meals at Buca di Beppo, the Italian restaurant. I asked Frank if he would go with me, and he said he would."

"That's great," interrupted Judy.

"No, it's not. At the last minute he said that his granddaughter had sneezed and he wanted to stay home to make sure she didn't get sick. Is that stupid or what? Sneezed, really! His daughter lives in that great big house with him and can take care of her daughter very well. She doesn't need Frank to watch Chelsea."

"You'd think that he'd make up a better excuse than that. I tell you, Carrie, the man is flaky. In fact, I think I'll call him Flaky Frank."

"He says that he's going to move in with me so that we can have more time together and see if we are compatible for marriage."

"Move in? Are you that serious about the guy?" Judy asked.

"Yes, I think so. I believe my living with him for a while will prove our compatibility. I am a little gun-shy after already having two marriages that weren't ideal."

"Are you going to let him move in?"

"Probably."

***

"I love living with you. I'm so comfortable here, and we have lots of good times. And I'm glad to be able to help you financially. I know you said that you just want gifts, but I would rather pay all your bills." Most of the time Frank was normal. He helped Carrie a lot. Besides, she liked to look at him. He had a very handsome facial bone structure, what some would call 'chiseled.'

"Yes, the last week has been lovely. And, Frank, you are wonderfully generous! I like taking care of you—cooking, cleaning, and so forth. In fact, you need help right now—let me straighten your glasses. They're crooked, or maybe it's your head that's crooked," Carrie joked. "Let me cut off your ear and even things up."

"*Don't...ever*...threaten me with knives." Shaking, Frank broke out in a sweat.

"I was just kidding."

"I don't care. You don't have any big knives around here, do you?"

In the morning Carrie had already forgotten about the weird exchange. She was on the way to Winn-Dixie to buy some goodies for a delicious meal she would prepare for Frank and herself.

When she came home, Frank's car was gone. That's strange; Frank never goes anywhere without me, she thought.

In the house she looked around for clues to his disappearance. She didn't have to look far when she found a note that said, "I have moved out. I don't like being threatened with knives." She raced into the bedroom. Sure enough, his clothes were gone from the closet. In fact, there was no trace that Frank had ever been there, which was eerie.

Carrie dialed Frank. She got his answering machine. "Frank, what's going on? I was only kidding. I would never hurt you. I love you."

After several calls with no response, Carrie decided to drive to his home. She pounded on the door. "Open up, Frank." She knew he was there because she could see his car in the garage. He never came to the door so Carrie returned home.

Carrie did not hear from Frank for five days although she left a message every day. On the sixth day, she answered the phone and heard, "Can I come back? I'm sorry. I thought it through and realized that you didn't intend to hurt me."

"Yes, come on back. I won't ever threaten you again, even in jest."

***

"How is Flaky Frank?" Judy was her usual curious self.

"Everything is perfect in love-land. Well, almost perfect."

"What do you mean 'almost perfect'?"

"There is no sex in our relationship. Frank can't perform."

"My God, Carrie. Why are you putting up with that?"

"I love him. He is so good to me. We do cuddle a lot, and I get my affection that way."

"I wouldn't settle for that. That's not sex."

"Well, you didn't go seven years in your first marriage without sex. You learn that you can get by without it."

"What? You mean that you and Bill had a sexless marriage?"

"No, we had wonderful sex for three years after we married. But then he started taking beta blockers and had no interest after that."

"My God, Carrie, they have a treatment for that problem."

"I know. I begged Bill to go get help. He said that he would but then never did. I was crazy about the man, and it just didn't matter. The marriage was great in every other way."

***

Carrie returned from buying a new dress to look sensational for their one-month anniversary of living together. However, Frank's car was gone again. "Where is he now?" Carrie wondered. Her heart began to pound, and her stomach turned over. She raced through the house and to the closet. His clothes were gone again. A note said that he couldn't handle the dog hair anymore.

Carrie knew that she wouldn't be able to get a call through to Frank. However, she left him a message. "You know that I keep our house impeccably clean. What dog hair are you talking about?"

After a few days Frank called again and begged to come back. "I won't leave again. I've learned my lesson—we're meant to be together. I love your dog. He doesn't really bother me."

Carrie took him back. "His luggage has frequent flyer miles," she thought.

One afternoon shortly after his return, Frank said, "My son, who's a doctor, wants me to get treatment in a clinic. He said that he wants his old dad back."

"What kind of clinic?" Carrie didn't know about a treatment for people with fear.

"A substance abuse clinic."

"You don't abuse any substances, do you, Frank?"

"Well, sort of. I take a lot of drugs. Don't get upset, Carrie. I don't buy them on street corners."

"Frank, if the doctor prescribes them, that's not substance abuse."

"It is if you get the same prescription drug, say for pain pills, from several doctors."

"Oh no, Frank, you do that?"

"Yes, I need them, and I can't get any one doctor to prescribe enough. Without them, I am in such pain."

"Well, I think you should take your son's advice and go for help."

"I'll consider it, but that means I'll be away from you for a couple of months."

"I'll be waiting when you get out."

***

Carrie continued to live with Frank and continued to encourage him to go for treatment. Their relationship was not ideal, to say the least. Four more times Carrie went somewhere and when she came home, Frank had moved out. He would always leave some inane note as to why. She would hope that he had gone for treatment, but he never had. She never ran after him any more. She just waited for his call wanting to come back.

Frank began again, "I'm so sorry, Carrie. You know I have a problem, and I get scared over things. Something freaks me. Please take me back."

"No, this time I can't do it, Frank. I just can't go on like this. You may be sick, but you're making me sicker. I have bad stomach spells every time you leave. Do you realize how awful it is for me to come home and find you gone? All trace of you, gone from my life."

***

"Do you really mean it?"

"Yes, Judy, I do. I can't take it anymore. And furthermore, no more drug addicts in my life! I think I will be able to recognize the flaky behavior the next time. You're so smart, Judy. Flaky Frank was a good name for him!"

I've Forgotten More Than You'll Ever Know About Him

"How do you find them, Carrie?

"What do you mean?"

"You find every weirdo in the world to date. I'll grant you that they seem okay on the surface, but each and every one of them has a gigantic flaw."

"I guess I'm looking for love in all the wrong places, Judy," Carrie said, laughing.

"I'm serious. Here you are—a very smart lady that had an outstanding career in a male-dominated field. Didn't you learn anything from all those men you worked with, or from your brothers, or from all the men in engineering school?"

"I guess I come across as very dumb or very needy, don't I?"

"You said it, not me."

"Well, anyway, I've decided to stop looking for Mr. Moneybags."

"Why's that?" Judy couldn't believe her ears.

"Mainly because I've met someone nice, and I don't think he has a pot to pee in."

"Where'd you meet him?"

"At an estate sale. He looked so handsome, sort of French, in his black turtle neck sweater. He has a big nose. You know I love big noses."

"At estate sales you're supposed to look at all the household items for sale, not look at or for men," Judy explained.

"Well, they have sales around here every Friday, and I always go to them. I don't exactly know why. I have a house full of stuff already. So I look but sometimes I get tired of looking at merchandise and start looking at the other people there who also probably have a house full of stuff."

"I suppose you went up to him and complimented him on his turtle neck shirt." Judy was always trying to get pointers on how to approach men she didn't know.

"Noooo, I flirted with him."

"How does a 55-year-old woman flirt?" Judy was laughing now at the picture this brought to mind.

"I caught his eye from across the room and didn't let go."

"Didn't let go?"

"You know, I kept looking at him much longer than I should have and then I smiled. Believe me, that makes men take notice."

***

At the estate sale the man sidled up to Carrie, introduced himself as 'Steve,' and struck up a conversation. After a while he asked, "Are you a dating lady?"

"Yes, I go out occasionally."

"How about going out with me tonight? I have to deliver some books and then we'll go catch dinner."

***

Dinner was at Denny's, but even though the restaurant wasn't fancy like Carrie "fancied" herself in, Steve and Carrie enjoyed themselves and hit it off right away. He was a very charming man. He wasn't French but seemed to have that continental charm. Actually, he was from Kentucky. Carrie laughed to herself about mistaking a Kentuckian for a debonair Frenchman.

"How come a handsome man like you is on the loose?"

"I'm divorced and am busy in my book store. I don't have much time to look for dates."

"Lucky me!" Carrie was sincere. She did consider herself lucky to find such a charming, down-to-earth guy.

They continued to date. The dates were never elaborate. They usually consisted of going to an estate sale or an auction to find old books, then to lunch or dinner, and then back to Carrie's house for a little lovin'. He taught

Carrie how to screw sideways, sort of at an angle, which she enjoyed. Steve always left near eleven o'clock at night. Carrie even asked him to stay over, but he always had an early appointment the next day.

She was excited that he agreed to be with her on Christmas Day, which was traditionally a very lonely day for Carrie. It was a day off for him so she figured he would be able to stay a long time. Not so; at three o'clock in the afternoon. he said that he had to go check on his mother.

***

"What makes you so damn smart, Judy? You don't even date much, and most of the time I think you know more about men and life than I do."

"I don't know. Lord knows, I can't run my own life."

That's true, Carrie thought, remembering that Judy is totally supporting her three adult children and six grandchildren.

"Well, Miss Smarty, tell me where Steve goes when he leaves me."

"I would say he has a wife. Ask to be invited to his home and watch him do the 'old soft shoe' to get out of having to entertain you in his home."

***

"Why don't we have dinner at your home tonight, Steve? Let's get carry-out. I would love to see your place."

"It's not much, but I'll take you there if you want." Steve lived in a gated condominium community in Sun View. There are big elaborate condos there and also smaller, much older, condos.

Steve is right. His tiny condo is not much, but at least he has one and at least he is willing to show it to me. The condo had one bedroom and a bath and a half. It was sparsely furnished with what appeared to be hand-me-down furniture. There were no traces of a woman—no makeup lying around, no female clothes, no bouquets of silk flowers, and no woman's touch in decorating. Judy was wrong for a change. He doesn't have a wife or a live-in girlfriend.

However, his pattern of leaving continued. Even on her birthday. Even on long weekends. Every date, he left much earlier than would be expected.

Carrie knew he didn't just stop by to screw her. He was always very considerate of her feelings and interested in her life. He always seemed like he regretted leaving her.

Out of the blue, one day Carrie began to think about his ex-wife. Steve had told Carrie her name only one time, but Carrie had remembered it. Carrie decided it must have been divine intervention but one day she had the thought that she should drive by the ex-wife's house after one of Steve's early departures. Her address was listed in the phonebook.

Oh no, his car's there, in front of her house! He's not even trying to hide it. So this is where he goes! He must be trying to get her back. Maybe he's just visiting her sons. He seems to be quite fond of them. Her mind was running wild now and trying to dream up plausible reasons why Steve would be at his ex-wife's house.

Carrie went right home and called the ex-wife's telephone number. This will settle it once and for all, she thought.

"Hi, may I speak to Steve, please?"

"Who is this?"

"Carrie Bolton. I'm Steve's girlfriend."

"Well, you may be his girlfriend, but I'm his wife."

"Wow! He said he was divorced," Carrie said.

"No, we're separated, but we're working on our marriage. Please leave him alone. Get your own man."

"This certainly explains his disappearances," Carrie said.

"Well, you explain his disappearances from this end," Steve's wife retorted.

***

Carrie was crying. Seeing Carrie cry, Judy's visiting grandchildren started to cry. Judy even started crying when she saw her grandchildren being so empathetic. Finally, they all started laughing and crying at the same time. Carrie was reliving the story for them. The children were all sitting on the floor around Carrie's knee while she spoke.

"I can't believe it! He was living a double life."

"I should have warned you, Carrie. All Kentuckians are liars. I've known several, and every last one of them was a liar. He may live down here now, but he's a Kentuckian through and through," Judy explained.

"I'm going back to men with money. At least I end up with something—memories of fun trips, jewelry, something—when it's all over. Aren't there any straight, nice, normal, unmarried men out there with a little extra cash?"

Judy wanted to know exactly where Carrie drew the line so she asked, "Why'd you mention "straight?" You haven't run into any gay men, have you?'

"Just gimme time," said Carrie. She was getting involved with every weirdo around so she figured a gay guy, not yet out of the closet, could be next.

The End of the World

"What makes you pick all the wrong men, Carrie?"

"Yeah, they all do seem so wrong, don't they?"

"Have you ever had a satisfactory relationship, Carrie?"

"I can't think of one."

"How about your father? What kind of relationship did you have with him?"

"Not good. He was aloof. He might as well have left me. He left me alone emotionally."

"That's the problem, Carrie. You pick men that will leave you, just like your father did. That's all you know. That's what love is like for you."

"Okay, stop the amateur psycho-babble."

"It's true, Carrie."

"Wait! I did have a perfect relationship once—my high school boyfriend Danny."

"And why aren't you with him now if it was so perfect?"

"He left me too. Okay, so maybe you have a point," Carrie admitted.

***

The mention of her high school boyfriend got Carrie to daydreaming of him that evening after Judy had left. She always tried to put him out of her mind but often sadly thought of him. He was a tall guy with a wonderful personality. Just the thought of him made her knees weak. She had always been so physically attracted to him. Maybe it was early hormones acting up, but he could always really turn her on.

If you like me like I like you,
I bet you by and by,
Our romance will be hotter
Than red flannels in July.

Carrie still remembered this verse from the first valentine Danny gave her in the third grade. She had been in love with Danny since the second grade when they had been instantly attracted to each other. Many would say that two seven-year-old kids can't have any chemistry, no love at first sight, but Danny and Carrie did. They just knew they belonged together.

Their relationship in grade school was all innocence. They rode their bikes up and down the streets of their Indiana hometown. Carrie guessed they were bike riding a lot as her Aunt Jean asked her mother, "Who is that boy I see Carrie with all the time?"

Every Saturday afternoon in junior high they went to the movies with a group of kids. Danny and Carrie always found each other in the crowd and would sit together. One day he put his arm around her in the movie and held her hand. Carrie didn't protest. She had a difficult time concentrating on the movie after that.

One's first kiss is always memorable. Carrie's was memorable but also messy. Danny and Carrie met at the town's annual Spring Fling. There were many games to play and much dancing. They took part in the Cakewalk. Danny stopped on the right square when the music stopped and won a big, tall chocolate cake. They couldn't figure out what to do with it, so like kids will do, they sat down on the curb and ate the cake. Carrie must have looked particularly fetching with chocolate icing all over her face and hands because Danny leaned over and kissed her. They sat there, eating cake, throwing cake, and kissing.

Danny and Carrie continued dating through high school. They never went steady with a ring but, nevertheless, went steady. They parked in deserted locations after every date to neck and pet. Carrie remained a virgin but a technical one. They pretty much did everything sexual except have intercourse. Carrie had big plans for her life and didn't want to get pregnant. Danny begged for more all the time. They never professed undying love, but they were devoted to each other.

Therefore, what happened next was very sad. They didn't have an argument. They didn't agree to part. They didn't agree to date others in college. They just drifted apart. They were both excited about going to college. They didn't think about the fact that there would be long absences, one from the other. They just assumed that they'd go on being a couple.

College life is very seductive. Carrie and Danny were both pulled into an environment of new friends, new interests, new goals, and new habits. Each of them found another person to share college life with—for Danny, it was a pretty teacher named Ellen and for Carrie, it was a veterinary student named Don. Carrie cried when she learned that Danny and Ellen married.

However, Carrie never thought that Danny's and her relationship was over. Carrie still would have dreams about him after many years had passed. Often they were happy dreams, but mostly they were about abandonment. At their class reunions, they talked as if over thirty years had not passed. He still had that loving look in his eye when he tapped her on the shoulder as he did so long ago. Ellen, Danny's wife, told Carrie that Danny suffered from frequent depression, but he never seemed depressed to Carrie at the reunions.

Carrie often wished things had turned out differently for Danny and her. She thought of her two marriages, one ending in a divorce and one happy marriage that ended with the death of her husband. With her second husband, Carrie moved to Sun View, Florida, to live in a retirement community. She loved all of the activities and took part in many of them. After his death, it always seemed as if something were missing from her life—someone to share her life with, she guessed.

***

One day in the drugstore Carrie looked up from a magazine she was skim reading. "Boy, that tall figure sure looks familiar, almost like Danny." Knowing that he was far away in Indiana, she returned to her magazine.

A little later, she felt a familiar tap on her shoulder. Whirling around, she said, "Oh my, it can't be! Danny, what are you doing in Sun View?"

"I'm in the process of moving here."

"Really! Do you remember that this is where I live now?"

Danny flashed a big smile. "Oh, I remember all right. That's why I moved here."

"Because of all the fun I mentioned?" Carrie just couldn't believe her ears.

"Well, partly. When Ellen died ten months ago, I wanted a new start. I have always loved Florida even though Ellen didn't. I just figured I would get my new start in Florida in a busy retirement community and possibly see you."

"Danny, I'm so sorry about Ellen. I heard that she had breast cancer, but everyone thought she had it beat."

"After her death, I kept thinking of how she just wasted away—an awful picture that I just couldn't get out of my mind. But I am here now—ready for a new beginning."

Carrie had had a recurring thought, through the years, that sometime, somehow, Danny and she would be together again. She daydreamed they would appear in a newspaper one day as two elderly people who had reunited after many years. It now looked like her daydreams were coming true on an earlier schedule! Right in Sun View!

Carrie and Danny began to renew their relationship. It didn't take long. In some ways it felt like no time had passed. They were deliriously happy. They just couldn't get enough of each other. They made love frequently. It was even better than what Carrie had dreamed of so often. The happiest day of her life was when Danny presented her with an engagement ring. She, of course, accepted right away his proposal of marriage.

"You know I have to go back to Indy to close on my house. I'll miss you, but I have to do it," Danny explained at breakfast one morning.

"I know. Do you want me to go with you?"

"No, I won't be long and then I'll be right back with you forever. Okay?"

"Okay."

Danny left. They talked each day on the telephone. Danny reported his progress in his real estate matters, but much of their conversations had to do with how lucky they felt to have finally got together and all their plans for their life together

***

Carrie raced to the phone as she did every evening. Danny was calling a little early this evening, she thought.

"Hello."

"Hello, Carrie?" It was Jim, Danny's brother.

"Hi, Jim, what's happening?"

"Carrie, I have some very bad news." Jim was choking up.

Jim, what is it?" Carrie had a sick feeling. Somehow she knew.

"Danny had a terrible car accident and was killed instantly."

Carrie went through the motions of getting the details, but she was actually in a trance. In fact, she was in a trance for days. She loved Danny so much and thought constantly of the chance they had finally had for happiness. She couldn't get over the fact that she came so close to pure, perfect love. The only thing that helped, at all, was her belief that maybe someday they would meet on the other side...somewhere over the rainbow.

If Loving You is Wrong, I Don't Want to be Right

"We meet again. Remember, the birthday party?" Tim asked Carrie as they were helping decorate Community Hall, a large building where various club's held their dances and other events. The hall held fifty tables but only forty when a dance floor was needed. Either amount of tables took a while to decorate so the whole dance committee had been asked to show up to decorate.

"Of course I remember you, Tim. It was fun meeting someone who also retired from Xerox, although from a different location. I don't think much about that workaday life anymore now that I am retired, but it was sort of fun reminiscing for a while."

Mostly Carrie remembered how handsome Tim looked at the birthday party. He didn't look old enough to be retired, but she knew he was, after their conversation. The men Carrie thought were handsome might not always be classically handsome, but they always had something different that set them off from the others, maybe it was a twinkle in their eye, a devastating smile; sometimes it was something indefinable. For Tim, it was his boyish good looks and charm. He looked like he had been Peck's bad boy when he was younger but too cute for the teacher to want to punish.

"This dance is going to be fabulous tonight. The committee has gone all out for it. I sort of wish that I were going," Tim was saying.

"I know—it seems silly not to go to the dance after being on the committee planning it, but I don't have a date," Carrie explained.

"What! You're not going either? Why don't we go together? It'll be great fun. We really should go."

"Ok, it's a date. Pick me up at 6:30, if you don't mind," Carrie said.

The dance was spectacular. The band was great, and the crowd was jumping. The dance was a Rock and Roll Revue so the band played all the oldies. Tim and Carrie could really jitterbug well and enjoyed showing off. When the slow dances came, they fell easily into each other's arms. Chemistry was beginning to cause sparks. Carrie was very attracted to Tim, and she could tell Tim was attracted to her too.

They were both disappointed when the band played the last number. "How about a drink? I know a late night club. It's in Riverview, but at this time of night we can get there pretty fast. I don't want our evening to end," said Tim.

At the club Carrie and Tim slid into the booth and sat close together. Their drinks arrived when they were already deep in conversation about Xerox.

Suddenly, Tim said, "I don't want to talk about Xerox anymore. I want to talk about us."

"What about us?" Carrie asked. Carrie could hardly contain her excitement. She wanted there to be an "us" discussion.

"I am very attracted to you. I think you're attracted to me. I just feel it. You are the kind of woman I've always dreamed of loving. To be blunt, I want to have an affair with you."

"Well, you certainly are straightforward! You mean that you're not involved with anyone else?"

Tim looked surprised. "Well, you know I'm married, don't you? I assumed you saw my wife at the birthday party."

Carrie's eyes filled with tears. "No, I had no idea. I didn't see you with anyone. There were so many people there. Why did you invite me to the dance? Why didn't you take your wife?"

"My wife and I just go through the motions of being married. All romance is gone. We respect each other, but that's it. I pretty much go my way, and she usually stays home. Every once in a while she will go somewhere with me, like the birthday party, but most of the time she is quite content to do nothing. I can't live like that so I get out and do things."

"Well, unfortunately, I am very attracted to you too. However, an affair is out of the question." Wanting to stop the tears and change the subject, Carrie said, "You know you should really try to revive your marriage as long as you respect her." It seemed to be working. Carrie continued trying to pull herself together by offering advice.

"No, the marriage is dead."

"You loved her at one time. Think back on all the things you loved about her when you married her. I can only be your friend, but I care enough about you to want to help you try to revive your marriage. Will you let me try? I know it's presumptuous of me, but I have had some experience."

Carrie wondered if she really wanted to help or did she just want an excuse to see Tim once a week as they agreed? Tim had suggested that they get together once a week to maintain their friendship. Carrie had jumped at the chance to see him so they would meet, and Carrie would give suggestions.

She had read "The Total Woman" a long time ago. It was a book in which the author purports that any marriage can be saved by following all of her easy steps. Mostly the steps consist of paying attention to the other person—listen when she talks, give compliments, buy gifts, plan little dates, don't criticize, don't nag, and start small physical contact such as holding hands. It was suggested that the execution of these steps be gradual, over many weeks.

Carrie and Tim had met for several months. "You know, Carrie, I think Josie is starting to respond to my efforts. She's seems much happier lately, and she certainly doesn't nag me very much anymore."

Carrie should have been happy. In fact, she acted elated, but secretly she was so much in love with Tim that she was having a tough time with his success. She had grown so close to him in their weekly visits. Her initial assessment was correct. He was a great guy. He was everything she wanted in a man. As he told her of his recent success, she realized it was never to be. She wished that she had just ended the whole relationship that night in the bar.

They continued to meet, faithfully every week. They had a standing date. On the one-year anniversary of their first and only real "date" Tim took Carrie to the little bar that they had gone to after the dance. After ordering drinks, Tim took Carrie's hands. "You know, this is never going to work. I have tried—for your sake, for Josie's sake, and for my sake. Josie and I are now very good friends. But that's all. There's no romance. There's no sex. I just don't love her anymore. I respect her as a wonderful person and the mother of my children. But I need more than that. And so does Josie. We have agreed to get a divorce.

Carrie was shocked. In her wildest dreams, she had hoped for this outcome but never imagined that it could really happen. Of course, she realized that he had not said anything about how she figures into these plans.

Tim said, "Once I get through my divorce, I want us to get a fresh start on our relationship. I am very much in love with you. This past year has just made me want you even more. I tried to put you out of my mind, but I couldn't. Let's continue to meet once a week until the divorce is final, okay?"

At their once-a-week meetings, Carrie would listen to divorce details. There was lots to think about, ending a 30-year marriage. The proceedings dragged on for weeks, even though it was a very friendly divorce. They had to have lots of discussions with the lawyers about the division of their property.

For one meeting with Carrie, Tim was late. Very late. This was so unlike him. When he finally slid into the booth in the seat across from her, Carrie could tell he was very upset. "What's wrong, Tim?"

"I just got back from the doctor's office. He asked me to come along for Josie's appointment."

"What happened? Are you all right?"

Cutting to the quick, Tim said, "Josie has Alzheimer's disease. She is just starting the middle stage. I thought that she was awful forgetful lately but then so am I. I just attributed it to old age. She would ask me the same question several times a day. For instance, she can never remember what day it is. It's her short-term memory. She's okay with stories from the past."

"Oh, my God. What are you going to do? You can't divorce her now, can you?"

"I know. The doctor said that she will need someone with her most of the time. I'm so sorry, Carrie. I'm sad, mostly for you. And for me. We could have had a wonderful life together; at least we were headed that way. I just can't leave her now. I'm all she's got. You understand, don't you, Carrie?"

Carrie was openly crying now. She was crying so much, she took a long time to regain her composure and respond, "Of course, I understand. I hate it, but I do understand. That's one of the many things I love about you. You are a very caring person."

"You know I won't be able to see you anymore. Not even for our once-a-week meetings. The doctor said that she will soon be in the "wandering" stage and could easily get lost. I can't leave her alone. I could call you, but I won't as I want to free you to seek someone else to love. I love you enough to do that for you."

***

"And you just parted?" Judy asked.

"We just parted. I'll always love him, but I have to respect what he's doing. And I have to respect myself and not get tied up in a situation that can last for years. Believe me, though, I cried myself to sleep for weeks."

If You've Got the Money, Honey, I've Got the Time

"Damn, Carrie, now you switched from dating weirdoes to dating men that break your heart in some tragic way."

"I know. I really think, Judy, that I'll just stop dating…or at least stop trying so hard to find someone. I think I will just reflect on the many memories I have had from a wonderful, if somewhat unconventional, life. I don't think I'm destined to find true lasting love. I'm not even sure it exists."

"How can you call your life 'wonderful'?" Your first marriage didn't sound so great. You've never told me much about it, but you did say that you totally supported him financially and that you had a sexless marriage for the last seven years. That right there is enough to make most women resign from ever wanting another man!"

"You don't understand, Judy. Nobody did. Those were the only two bad things about him. Everything else was wonderful. I tried to explain it to my parents after he left me."

"Mother said to me 'When are you going to stop crying and get angry? Bill didn't treat you very well and then he had the nerve to leave you. You need to go to the doctor and get a short-term antidepressant. You've been crying for three weeks. Also, maybe some day you will explain to your father and me what you saw in him!'"

"Well, I tried to explain it to them, Judy. They needed first to understand where I was in my life when I met Bill. I was very successful in my career, knocking down more money than most professional men. I didn't want for anything. I had a beautiful home, beautifully decorated, and a luxury car. I was very happy. I had plenty of close friends. I entertained a lot, traveled a lot, and had lots of boyfriends, usually one at a time. However, I felt something was missing in my life, and I came to the conclusion that it was a husband. After all, my friends were all married."

Judy spoke up. "It's probably a subject of another discussion why you had never found anyone to marry. I've seen pictures of you—you were very attractive."

"The men I fell for were not marriage-material or didn't want to get married. The ones that wanted to marry me didn't measure up, in my eyes. I once made an idle comment to a girlfriend, 'If only I could buy a husband.' Boy, did that come true!"

"When I least expected it, Bill entered my life. I took a girlfriend, who was quite shy, to a singles bar to find a man for her. The bar was very crowded, and Bill offered us seats at his table where he sat alone. I assessed right away that Bill was intelligent, courteous, reasonably attractive, extremely funny, and a very good conversationalist. He took turns dancing with my friend and me. When it was time to go, he walked both of us to our cars. When he saw my late-model Cadillac, he lost his cool and said, 'Wow, is that yours?' That should have been a tip-off; in fact, it was."

"I knew right from the beginning that Bill liked the fact that I was financially independent. Bill and I were together constantly for one year. During that time he continued to be an intelligent, considerate, and very funny companion. My friends all loved him and considered me to be very lucky. He made them feel important by being a very good listener and a witty conversationalist. At the end of our first year together, we married in a lovely candlelit ceremony in front of 300 friends and family."

Bill just had one flaw as I saw it—he did not like to work. He felt, although he never said as much, that he was born to be an executive and did not want to start at an entry-level job. He was smart enough to be an executive, but business and industry don't work that way. You either have to inherit a business or work your way up. I would have liked him to work, not because we needed the money, but because it was difficult when my friends asked me what Bill did for a living."

"Many times he had some "hot" idea, always trying his hand at something to make money. His schemes never worked, because he never worked. At least, it gave me something to tell my friends that Bill did. However, in all cases, it ended up that I would have to buy him out of the situations."

"No matter how much money he cost me, I was crazy about the man. He was funny, and I love to laugh. He had an unusual ability to make funny, if not hilarious, comments about everyday life. He was a good lover, at least for the first three years, and enjoyed the same things I did—travel, country club socializing, nice clothes, entertaining, dining out, and all good things that money could buy. He never gave me reason to question his whereabouts and never flirted with other women."

"I never resented the fact that he didn't work but liked to spend my money. It seemed like the perfect situation—I got a perfect husband by paying the bills. As a counselor told me once, 'There are all sorts of husband-wife relationships out there. If you're comfortable with yours, it's okay.' We were comfortable, even very happy, for several years."

"When I was suddenly given an early retirement by Xerox, we needed to "downsize" our lifestyle. One thing that seemed obvious to me was that I needed to get rid of our big house we owned in a very exclusive gated community. Even though we moved into a very charming, lovely condo on the water, Bill said he felt closed in. I didn't give the comment much thought as I was busy starting a new, demanding job—one where I didn't know the people, the business, or the tasks required to perform the job but had to perform anyway. I would come home at night and collapse. I was too tired to pay much attention when Bill told me he wanted to start a real estate career."

"But Frankie paid attention. She assured him that he was right in wanting to go into real estate, that I was not being supportive, and that he was such a wonderful person."

"Who's Frankie?" Judy interjected.

"Frankie and Bill had been casual friends for about two years. Being a shop owner in a small town, she would be the only gal who would meet with the guys having coffee at Burger King every morning. Bill loved to regale the guys and her with his funny stories. When she decided to divorce her husband, Bill became her next target. It was not difficult to envelop him in an affair. He was getting very little attention at home, and she was putting him on a pedestal."

"I discovered the affair almost immediately, because he started acting different than he ever had—staying out late, having cryptic telephone conversations, etc. When I confronted him, he readily admitted the affair, broke down crying, and said, 'I didn't mean to fall in love with her. I love you both.'"

"I, of course, begged him to give her up and come back to me. I even explained all of the advantages I had over her."

"Silly you," Judy said.

"But that's what you do when you're desperate. Bill said, 'She understands me because she is just like me. She has no self-esteem either. You deserve much better than me, Carrie.'"

"Friends, family, my minister, and my attorney all tried to console me. They had a difficult time because they never quite understood the complicated relationship that we had. I'm not even doing a good job of explaining it now. Friends said that he used me, but I used him just as much. My minister offered, 'A marriage will never work if the woman makes more money than the man.'"

"My attorney said that I should grant Bill's request for a large amount of money in the settlement. 'I will twist your arm until you take that offer. That's the best deal you'll ever get. Don't you realize that he is actually entitled to half of your condo, half of your savings, half of your securities, and worst of all, half of your Xerox retirement?'"

"I took his offer, somewhat begrudgingly. I felt I'd paid enough for ten years, but the lawyer was very adamant. And, thus, Bill and I parted. I can say, though, that I'm not sorry for the ten years with Bill and would do it all over again. I consider them wonderful years with many great, fun-filled memories."

"Now, Judy, aren't you sorry you asked? Can't you see why I'm looking for a man to love me and spend a little money on me?"

"Yes, I guess so, but frankly I would just be worn out."

"It did take me a couple of years to recover."

Stand By Your Man

"Have you ever dated any guy more than a few months? You know some people are okay after you get to know them," Judy commented to Carrie.

"Judy, puh-leeze, these guys all have serious problems, but yes, I did date one guy, Bob, for four and one-half years when I was younger, in my early single years. That was before I knew to get out fast when a problem arises," Carrie explained.

"Why, what happened with Bob?"

"Wait 'til I tell you. You're not going to believe this one. It happened when I lived in Baltimore."

"I met Bob in Annabelle's, a bar used by the single set for meeting people. 'You're pretty cute,' he said. "He was pretty cute too, in a big sort of way. He must have been 6'4" and big around, not fat, just big."

"That's a straightforward pickup line, if I ever heard one," I said with a twinkle in my eye.

"I don't mess around," Bob explained.

"Thus started a four and a half-year love affair. Bob was just about everything I wanted in a man. He was tall and pretty good-looking, very bright, and had a terrific job. He was just 38 years old but was already Deputy Director of a large federal government facility in Baltimore. Bob was a lawyer by training but now operated as the right-hand man to the director of this installation, which employed thousands of people."

"We started dating exclusively very quickly although I would only see him about twice a week due to the demands of our careers. We cooked dinner and watched TV a lot, just wanting to take it easy and relax from our stressful jobs. Occasionally, we went out to dinner or attended parties at friends' homes. I taught Bob to play bridge, which he took to immediately and became quite good. In September we spent every weekend and several weekdays in Ocean City, Maryland, where he owned a condo right on the ocean."

"Bob was very good to me, fun to be around, and very stimulating as his intellect was as fine as I had ever encountered. He was a man's man. There was no pushing Bob around. I had to be careful and not be too assertive. He considered me an equal and allowed me to pay my own way, something I insisted on, but making too many demands on his emotional life was off limits, I soon learned."

"Within six months we talked of marriage but not with the outcome I'd hoped for. He explained that he could never marry me. He was separated from his wife and planned on divorcing her. However, because he was a Catholic, he could never marry again without getting an annulment of his first marriage, something he didn't want to do as he and his wife had three children. I, of course, thought by being Miss Wonderful, by being everything he ever wanted in a woman, I'd be able to change his mind. Wrong! I tried for four and one-half years but did not succeed and ended up leaving him for this reason and several others."

"His relationship with his wife bothered me some. He still lived at home but slept on the sofa. He did this for the children, so he said. He explained that his wife was very selfish. She knew about the "woman on North Charles Street," as I was called, but gave him no grief about me. She knew about me, but she didn't know what I looked like, so I enjoyed observing her at the health club where we both worked out. She was beautiful and looked like a young Elizabeth Taylor, complete with lavender-colored eyes. She did seem selfish to me and obsessed about her looks. Maybe Bob was right on this one."

"I considered his wife the least of my worries. What bothered me much more was the emotional distance that Bob kept between him and me. It is very difficult to explain. He never let me know ahead of time when we were going to do something. It was like he didn't want to tell me of his plans in case a better offer came along. Although he spent a lot of time with me and didn't date others, he never told me that he loved me. In fact, he never complimented me on anything except my job and my humor, mainly because I caught on to his intellectual wit."

"On the other hand, Bob was the center of my existence. I lived to hear from him or be with him. Nothing else mattered much to me. Oh, I held down a very good job with lots of responsibility, but that was necessary for survival, sort of like food, water, sleep, and shelter. I realize now that I was way too needy for my own good. The ultimate example is the following event. I will tell you, Judy, just as it happened."

***

"I stopped by Bo's last night, and he told me about a party that he's going to attend and wants us to attend, too," Bob explained, somewhat apprehensively. Bo had been Bob's best friend for several years. He was divorced and was quite the ladies' man.

"Well, that sounds good. I'm always up for a party. Who's having it?"

"A dentist whom Bo knows is having the party at his house. However, there's something you should know about this party."

"What's that?" I assumed that he was going to tell me that there'd be a lot of pot smoking at the party.

"There will be people there having sex, an orgy, you know."

"Oh, no, I'm not going to anything like that. That's just too bizarre—watching people have sex in front of other people. No sir."

"We discussed it at great length, but Bob ended by saying, 'Well, I am going; you can think about it more and let me know. I think it could be interesting. You know everyone now is into orgies.'"

"I had read a lot about the orgies that were going on. I never thought that I'd have to make this decision, though. Unfortunately, I was so insanely in love with Bob that I felt I couldn't let him go to the orgy by himself. What if he met someone else? What if he left me for her?"

"The night of the party came, and I was running late, on purpose I suppose. We arrived at the party after it had started and were ushered down the basement which had very plush carpeting. My, God, everyone is naked and having sex, was my first reaction. I'd thought there'd be just a few isolated cases of coupling, maybe in some remote bedrooms. Everyone was on the floor. It was as if it were forbidden to stand up. We got on the floor. Bob immediately took off his clothes. I immediately crawled to the pool table and hid behind it, occasionally peeking around to see what Bob was doing. I was horrified to see him with the prettiest girl in the room, rubbing her breasts.

"I was trying to decide what I was going to do about the situation when the naked host crawled up to me. 'Hi, I'm Dr. Mike; what's your name?'"

"I gave him my first and last name. (This was a big mistake I learned when the dentist called me for weeks afterward, trying to get a little 'one on one,' so to speak.) 'We don't use last names here,' he gently explained. It seems he took a liking to me and wanted to have sex. I told him I was sick, which, by now, was the truth. I crawled on the floor, not wanting to make a scene by standing up, to the bathroom and promptly threw up several times. Everyone left me alone as I hung onto the toilet bowl for the rest of the evening."

"The next couple of weeks were hell. I had many emotions that I'd never had before. I was ashamed of myself for going. I was jealous of Pilar, the gal with whom Bob made love on the floor, two times so he said. I was mad at Bob for enjoying himself. Bob thought that the whole evening was a hoot, so I dreaded the fact that he was going to want to go again. Bob felt he needed to tell me that it was okay for me to have sex at the orgies. He just didn't want me to do anything with Bo, his best friend. That seemed like a strange request to me!"

"Off we went again. The sick ploy worked so well that I tried it again and was successful. No one bothered me. I overheard someone ask Bob why he bothered to bring me. I wish I could say that the second party was the end. It was, sort of."

"Bob decided he liked switching partners with just one other couple better than an orgy. We tried this a couple of times. One memorable evening was spent with a German couple. We were all on a full-size bed, having sex to German military march music, when the bed crashed to the floor. Another night was spent with Pilar and her studly husband. He had a dick that was so long it gave me gas. This guy's "studliness" was lost on me; I was busy being jealous of Pilar, as Bob was particularly fond of her."

"Finally, I had had it! I couldn't stand the life I was leading. I picked a fight with Bob, and he left. I thought that he'd realize that this orgy life was driving me, Miss Wonderful, away, that he'd come to his senses, and that he'd come back. He never did."

"I moped around Baltimore for another year, living to accidentally run into Bob somewhere. I finally realized that this was ridiculous. Knowing that I would never be able to get him out of my mind in Baltimore, where everything reminded me of him, I decided that the time had come to go home to Indianapolis. I moved there and began a new life, free of orgies and other East Coast decadent behavior."

"When I told a psychiatrist that everyone on the East Coast was into orgies, he explained that he had lived on the East Coast and that he had never been to an orgy. This is how twisted my thinking had become...while adrift on a lonely sea."

How Many Arms Have Held You?

"I met an interesting guy last night, Judy."

"Who's that?"

"His name is Peter, and I met him square dancing. You know square dancing is very popular in Sun View as are most forms of dancing. There's ballroom dancing in which the ladies wear beautiful dresses. There's line dancing which is of interest to a lot of the widows so that they can do some dancing without a partner at the town's big dance events. Also, other dancing types of interest to the ladies are clogging and tapping. Square dancing clubs meet several times a week. The ladies dress in their big full skirts with crinolines, and the guys wear jeans, western shirts, and string ties."

"Sounds like you learned all about it. Back to Peter, did he dance with you?"

"Yes, but he danced with everyone. I'm sort of new to square dancing, but I think he was called an 'angel'," Carrie explained. "An angel is a guy who comes and dances with some of the gals who are just learning to dance."

"That's nice."

"I might have it wrong, though. He just might be a guy who comes without a dance partner."

"Do you have a date with him?"

"No, but he talked a lot with me. I think he is sniffing me out."

"What do you mean?"

"Well, he was asking me a lot of questions about what I like to do in Sun View. He lives here too and thinks that it's a wonderful place because of all the activities."

"Did he mention what activities he likes?"

"He's into all sorts of things. It didn't sound like he misses much. I was particularly interested in the fact that he likes to play bridge. In fact, I told him that I also like to play bridge, and he suggested that we play together sometime."

"Why don't you just square dance with him?"

"Oh no, he is on a much higher level than I am. The advanced dancers don't like to be slowed down by beginners. That's why they have different level of classes and dances."

"Okay, that makes sense."

"However, I will check him out if he ever comes as an angel again."

***

"How's my favorite beginner?"

"Peter, how are you? I was wondering if you would be here again tonight."

"I do help out a lot. It's a great way to meet new people, just like I met you."

"Have you been playing any bridge?" Carrie asked.

"I play once a week with Seth, but that's pretty much all I can fit into my busy schedule."

"How about you?" Peter asked Carrie lots of questions, but he always looked around the room as he talked with her.

"I'm not playing much bridge, because I can't find a decent partner." Carrie was hinting that they should play bridge together. She felt that Peter was a pretty good player. At least, that's what he led her to believe, and she wasn't too bad herself.

Instead, Peter surprised her by asking her to a singles dance on Friday night. Carrie readily accepted although she thought it was odd to have a date at a singles dance.

***

"This is a really good singles dance. Lot of singles and a pretty even ratio of men to women. It's definitely not as good as the Sarasota dance, though, but that's 30-40 minutes away. I don't like to drive that far too often, so I just come to this dance which is one of my favorites here in town."

Carrie and Peter danced to several songs. After he led her back to the table, he asked her if she would like some punch or coffee.

"Yes, I would love to have some punch, but I can get it."

"No, stay seated. I'll get it for you," Peter said, appearing to be a real gentleman.

Carrie enjoyed listening to the music and watching the dancing. There was a nice crowd, probably 50-60 seniors. She couldn't get over how much dancing there was in Sun View. There had to be at least two to three dances going on a week.

After sitting for ten minutes, Carrie began to wonder what happened to Peter. They must have run out of punch, she thought. All of sudden, she looked at the dance floor, and there was Peter dancing with another woman. At first she thought that he must have run into an old friend. However, after sitting another twenty minutes with no punch and watching Peter whirl several other ladies around the floor, she was definitely puzzled. She wondered why he had brought her as a date.

"Miss me?" Peter appeared at the table with two glasses of punch.

"Well, I did sort of wonder what happened to you." Carrie was trying not to be angry. After all, maybe Peter just brought her to introduce her to this particular singles dance, which she'd never attended before.

"You should get up and dance with some others. Do a line dance or two."

"I usually let a man ask me to dance."

"Take advantage of the ladies choice dances and grab some handsome man."

The evening continued, and the pattern continued. Peter would dance several dances with Carrie and then he would disappear and dance with several other ladies.

On the way home, Carrie made up her mind that she would never go out with Peter again. Then he asked, "Will you go to church with me Sunday?"

Carrie had a lot of thoughts running through her mind. She thought she liked a man who is decent enough to go to church. And he probably won't leave me for another woman at the church, she thought. "Okay, I'll go. Which one do you attend?"

"United Methodist Church."

"Oh, good. I've been wanting to visit that church. Yes, I'll be glad to go with you Sunday."

On Sunday they arrived at the church about twenty minutes before the service and stood in the Narthex instead of being seated right away. Almost immediately a steady stream of women came up to Peter and talked with him. They all seemed to know him quite well. Peter was very mannerly and introduced Carrie to each one of them. He would make a point of saying something nice about each one. "She's a really good dancer." Or "She's a very energetic bike rider." Or "she's a life master at bridge." Carrie felt she had met half of the female population of Sun View.

After the service, on the way out, the same thing happened—many women appeared out of nowhere. Peter certainly knows lots of women, but surely he hasn't dated them all, she thought.

Peter took Carrie to Denny's for lunch after church. They had a nice conversation. At one point Peter asked about her marriages. She then in turn asked Peter about his. He told her about his one marriage that ended after 20 years. He said he really tried to make it work. He identified himself as a "recovering Catholic."

"So you know I didn't want a divorce, being a Catholic and all, but it couldn't be helped."

"Would you ever get married again, Peter?"

"Hell no. Once is definitely enough. Besides I have a saying, "Why give up the admiration of many for the scorn of one? Also, my favorite joke goes like this: 'Hey Bob,' said Bill, 'did you know a lot of shrinks say that sex on the first date can prohibit any truly meaningful and lasting relationship from ever developing?' Peter chuckled as he revealed the punch line: 'Darn right!' replied Bob. 'I count on it.'"

Carrie laughed out loud and to herself. Okay, now I've got his number. I understand where he's coming from.

***

"How's your romance going with Peter?" Judy hadn't heard very much about him lately and wondered what was happening.

"Oh, that's over. And it never was a romance."

"What happened? I thought he was a neat guy."

"He is a neat guy and in fact, we are best friends. However, he's definitely not for me. He has way too many girlfriends. We didn't click as lovers but definitely clicked as friends."

"Don't tell me you slept with him!"

"No, no. I didn't sleep with him. Didn't even think of it. We only had two dates. Even though you may not believe it, I don't sleep with men right away. I wait until I am really emotionally involved with them."

***

Peter and Carrie did become fast friends. Peter felt like he could tell Carrie pretty much anything. Carrie kept his secrets. She would always kid him about all of his women, and she got a kick out of his telling her of close calls when one gal would almost find out about another.

He always stopped short of telling her about his sex life, though. She would kid him about sleeping with all of the women. However, he told her over and over that he did not sleep with nearly as many as she thought. He said that he pretty much narrows the field down to one before he sleeps with her. He explained how sleeping with a lady brings on a whole different set of pressures that he didn't want unless she was really special.

One day when Peter called, he sounded upset. "What's wrong, Peter?

"I've just been to the doctor. Guess what? I'm going to have to give up my lifestyle I fear."

"What happened?" Carrie couldn't imagine what was wrong.

"I have a sexually transmitted disease, as they call it. I can't figure out who gave it to me. I am so careful, and I don't even sleep with many women."

"I understand that there's quite a bit of it in Sun View," Carrie offered. She had been to lunch with a friend who is a nurse and works in a Tampa clinic. "Someone who works in a clinic told me that they treat a lot of people in this town for Herpes, Clamidia, Syphilis, and other STDs."

"I guess I'm just going to have to give up sex. In all my years I've never had any problems. I just don't get it. All the ladies I date are not the promiscuous types."

"My nurse friend went on to say that the problem started when Viagra came out. It seems that the husbands are using the Viagra with hookers, not with their wives."

"Well, I don't ever use a hooker. How could that affect me?"

"All it takes is for an infected man to give up his hookers and have sex with one of the nice ladies you date."

"This is certainly putting a damper on things."

"Actually you're lucky. At least you can be cured with antibiotics. What is really serious is AIDS."

"Please, there's no AIDS in Sun View."

"Oh yes there is, according to my friend. She said that the guys in town use the whores in Olympic Beach. Several of them have AIDS, so there are several cases of AIDS in our little town."

Peter got rid of his problem. Carrie was glad and hoped that he would be a little more careful. She was really quite fond of Peter and didn't want anything to happen to him. She was really glad that she had quickly realized that Peter had a 'commitment phobia' and kept from committing by dating several women at once. Carrie was definitely not into sharing her men.

Make the World Go Away

"You were in the Navy for a couple of years after college, Carrie. Right? You must have met lots of eligible men then. Wasn't there anyone you were interested in?" Judy still couldn't figure out why Carrie never married until she was thirty-five.

"No, Judy, not really." Carrie couldn't decide whether to fill Judy in on her love affair in the Navy. She didn't think she'd understand. It did make Carrie start reminiscing though, and she decided to take a chance and tell Judy the story…

***

The instructor always spoke very precisely. "Ladies, this weekend, you have your first eight-hour leave. Let me remind you that you are still in training. You are not officers yet. This means, and may I be perfectly clear on this matter, there is to be absolutely, I repeat, absolutely, no fraternization with enlisted men, male officers, or male candidates, even if you recognize them as being from one of the other classes on this base. Most of you will probably go into Newport. There will be lots of military men roaming around, enjoying the sights just as you will."

Carrie's hand shot into the air.

"Yes, Bolton, what is it?"

"Lt. Starkey, what if the men hit on us, you know, approach us?"

"You are to ignore them. If they persist, you are to quote the Uniform Code which says that, and I paraphrase, 'male and female enlisted personnel shall not fraternize while in training.'"

Carrie thought this summer was going to be a bore without any men, but she was resigned to the rules. She and a couple of candidates in her class headed into Newport. They ate at a fancy restaurant for lunch. It was great to have something to eat besides the slop they were fed in the mess hall. After lunch, her two companions wanted to take a walking tour of Newport. Carrie was too tired for that. She was just getting used to the running, marching, and calisthenics she had to do in training. She didn't want any more exercise. They all parted company.

Carrie decided to stop in a creamery for dessert. A Rhode Island classmate had told her that she shouldn't miss having a hot fudge sundae at the creameries Newport's famous for. She didn't want a table all by herself, so she sat in the one remaining counter seat.

"Hi, I'm Pat Healey," her counter companion said immediately, "a good old Irish name."

"My name's Carrie Bolton. I see you're in training also."

"Yes, I started a month ago. It's rough, isn't it?"

"Yes, it's rough, and I don't see why I can't date," Carrie said, still with men on her mind. She flushed, embarrassed. She realized her comment made it sound like she was man-crazy.

Carrie and Pat had a long, leisurely talk, mostly about training. Pat was very good-looking, with brown hair with a red tint and beautiful brown eyes that mesmerized Carrie. *Oh, great, the first officer candidate I meet, and I'm already attracted. Oh, well, we'll never meet again. No harm done.*

"I can't stay here much longer today but would you meet me here next weekend? We can do some things together, like sightseeing, lunch at the counter, you know, spend some time together without really being together. So we don't give anyone the wrong idea," Pat quickly added. "We hit it off well, don't you think? I don't know about you, but I'm very lonely. I could use a friend like you." Pat's puppy-dog eyes looked soulfully at Carrie.

Carrie was lonely too. She was lost, in fact. A high school romance had gone sour after many years, and in college she was too busy to date much. "Okay, it sounds like fun. I can't be here until eleven a.m. 'cause we have morning inspection," Carrie explained.

"Oh, I remember that only too well." They went their separate ways back to the Naval Station.

Another week of training went by, and finally it was the weekend. Nothing had happened to cancel leave. Every one in the company had been on her good behavior so as not to jeopardize the precious time away from the base.

Pat and Carrie met at the creamery just as they had planned. They sat side by side at the counter. The two found they had a lot in common. They talked and laughed the afternoon away. Having been in town for a month, Pat had heard about all the good places to eat. They shared a couple bottles of wine and dinner at one of the spots, a very dark, small, out of the way, bistro-like restaurant.

After a meal of spaghetti and meatballs, Carrie said she guessed she should be heading back to base. Pat stroked Carrie's hand affectionately and said, "I want to be with you again next weekend. You know I'm very fond of you. Will you join me? I've something special in mind."

Carrie hesitated and then said, "You know I'm enjoying our time together as much as you are, but I'm afraid people will start talking about our being together often. I feel there are classmate spies everywhere."

Pat said, "I know. I worry about that too. And I can't afford to be thrown out of the military, which is the punishment if we're caught. I disappointed my father by flunking out of Annapolis, and I just couldn't stand to disappoint him again. He's my idol."

Pat continued, "I've a plan. Next week let's meet again at the creamery but not sit together. After we have lunch, you follow me. I'll lead you to a place where we can be safe and secure."

Carrie couldn't wait for the week to pass. In her room she didn't want her roommate to talk to her. She wanted to daydream about Pat. In fact, she kept to herself a lot now. This gave her plenty of time for fantasizing. She was now telling herself that she was falling in love with Pat. She wasn't sure whether Pat felt the same way, but she had caught some good vibes.

After inspection, Carrie headed downtown alone. Sure enough, there was Pat, sitting in the usual spot at the counter. Carrie chose to sit at a table for a change. Pat looked her way and smiled. After the meal Pat walked by Carrie's table and dropped some keys. Bending over to pick them up, Pat said in a hushed voice, "Remember the number, 407."

Carrie memorized 407, wondering what sort of place she was being taken to, but started following Pat about 100 feet behind. They walked down several streets before arriving at The Viking Hotel. Pat went in and got on the elevator.

Carrie started shaking. "Oh, my God, Pat has a room, Number 407." It didn't take her long to put two and two together. Carrie knew this was wrong, that she was taking a big chance, but she couldn't help herself. She loved Pat. She knew what was coming. She was already getting sexually aroused. She walked into the hotel and went right away to the elevator.

She got off at Floor 4 and went to Room 407. The door was ajar. Carrie went in and fell into Pat's arms. Their kiss was at first gentle and then passionate. The afternoon was spent in lovemaking as they explored every curve of each other's bodies. They were so consumed by passion that very little was said. Pat finally ventured, "You know, Carrie, this is against the rules."

"I know." Carrie didn't care. She was so deliriously happy. She loved Pat. She couldn't get enough of Pat. "And I also know that next weekend we get our first twenty-four hour leave. Just think, we can spend an entire day together, making love over and over again. Can you handle that?" Carrie asked as they were preparing to part.

"I can if you can." Pat smiled and let Carrie leave first. As Pat left, a couple of officer candidates in class were at the end of the hall. *Oh no, I hope they didn't see me!*

The weekend came and was pretty much a repeat of the previous weekend, including dropped keys and a whispered room number. By now Pat and Carrie were declaring undying love. They made plans to ask for Washington, D.C. as their first assignments. They knew if they both asked for D.C., they were bound to both get it as the Navy stationed a lot of junior officers there, and most did not want the duty nor request it. As officers, they could then live together and be seen together. Life would not have to be so furtive.

Carrie was so happy as she headed for the mess hall for breakfast she wanted to kick her heels in the air. She daydreamed constantly about her life with Pat. At long last, she wouldn't be lonely anymore. Finally she had found a soul mate, someone who understood her completely. She was in love. None of this training nonsense upset her anymore. She just did what she was told. She admitted to herself that studying was difficult as she always had Pat on her mind, but she did well enough to be in the top half of her class, so far.

The mess hall seemed livelier than usual. In fact, there was a buzz all around, and various girls were whispering to each other. Carrie asked a friend, "What's going on?"

"Haven't you heard? There's been a suicide. Someone jumped off the Newport/Pell Bridge."

Carrie tried to get more of the details. "Who was it?"

Her friend said, "That's what we're trying to figure out. All we know is that it was an officer candidate."

"Someone in our class?"

"No, someone in a class ahead of us."

Carrie finished her breakfast. She realized one of the classes ahead of hers was Pat's. She wished she could talk to Pat and get some information. Pat would know who it was."

On the way out of the mess hall, Carrie heard a group talking about the suicide. As she joined the group, she heard them say that the body had been identified, that it was Officer Candidate Pat Healey. Carrie was stunned. Her stomach turned over so many times she thought she was going to vomit. She felt dizzy as she asked, "Are you sure? Are you sure it wasn't an accident?" She was devastated. What should she do? She couldn't bust out crying like she felt like doing. There surely must be some sort of mistake. Pat loved her and wouldn't commit suicide. They were so close to permanent happiness. She felt she needed to find out for sure, but she couldn't let them know she knew Pat.

A class mate continued, "It was Healey, all right; the name tag was still in place. I guess Pat couldn't take it any longer. Classmates had gone to the Commanding Officer and told her that Pat was shacking up with a woman in a Newport hotel on leave. You know homosexuality is outlawed in the Navy. That would have been the end of her career. A note she left behind was some sort of an apology to her father."

Carrie wondered if they would ever find out that <u>she</u> was Pat's lover. She was nervous because if they did, she would be put out of the military. But mostly, Carrie was sad. *Why, Pat, did you do it? We were so much in love. Didn't that mean anything to you? Didn't you care how devastated I would be?*

She moped around, crying often. Her grades dropped. Somehow she managed to graduate and was commissioned an officer. Nothing was ever the same though. She lost her love for the service and thought she was even losing her patriotism. Most of all, she felt God was punishing her for having an affair with a woman. *God, is it such a terrible sin for me to love a woman?* Carrie would never have imagined that Lesbian love could be so sexually satisfying either. She had never thought about sex without a penis. She had learned something with Pat—a well-placed tongue was actually more satisfying than a cock. Men had performed cunnilingus on her before but had never brought her to climax that way.

The weeks and months went by. Time passed but not Carrie's pain. That lasted a lifetime.

I Didn't Promise You a Rose Garden

"I'm so sick of the single life. Not that I want to get married. I'm disgusted with what we have to go through just to get a date," Carrie complained to Judy.

"I heard the other day that there're a thousand dogs in Sun View. Maybe there're a lot of lonely people like you and me and they get a dog so they can receive a little affection. Why don't you get another dog, double the puppy love? That's what I'm ready to do. Something cute and cuddly, who will be so happy to see me and lick my face when I come home," Judy said and laughed.

"Now that is pathetic! Carrie loved her dog, but he certainly wasn't a substitute for a man. "Your suggestion, though, is not much stranger than what I had to endure the other Sunday afternoon."

"Another creepy blind date?" Judy asked.

"No. I heard about a lecture that Dr. Thornborough was giving. It was especially designed to teach senior singles how to open up for romance. It was being sponsored by one of the singles clubs in town."

Judy was impressed. "She's that noted psychotherapist who's hot on the local talk show circuit right now, isn't she?"

"Right, but I think she's kookier than most of her patients."

"What happened?" Judy didn't understand how a lecture could be that strange.

"Well," Carrie slowly explained, "this was a lecture with audience participation. Dr. Thornborough would talk for a while and then she had exercises for the audience to do. I have blocked out most of them, but I do remember one—we all had to get down on our hands and knees, the ones that could, in our good clothes, mind you, and go up to other audience members and bark like dogs."

"Wow, what was the point of that?" Judy was flabbergasted.

"The exercise, I think, was to lessen our inhibitions. You know, to put us all on a level playing field—everyone looked equally ridiculous. I'm never going to another singles lecture again. I wanted to leave in the worst way, but I didn't want the good doctor to make a comment as I left, as she did to another poor soul."

"I'm sorry, Carrie."

"Don't feel sorry for me, Judy. Live and learn, I always say." Carrie continued. "I've dated an alcoholic and a prescription drug addict, getting involved, in each case, before I knew what was going on. I fell in love with a guy who was into orgies. I've also spent way too much time on one who was still hung up on the wife that dumped him. The list goes on and on. I don't consider myself expert at anything in this life, but as far as dating goes, I've definitely earned a Ph.D. in the school of hard knocks."

"Do you want to try one more time? This Friday night there's a singles get-together. They're sponsoring a guy who's giving tips on maintaining cars. Even if we don't meet any men, we could learn something."

"No way! I've had it. I'm going to stay home with a good book," Carrie retorted.

"Come on. You always say if you had your life to do over, you would learn how a car works and how to take care of it. You know how you always feel you're getting taken at the repair shop." Judy was pleading now.

"Oh, okay. I'll go, but I'm not talking with anyone. I'm just going to sit there and listen. I'm not getting involved with anyone. I'm going only because you're my best friend. Let's go in separate cars, though, so once you're smitten with some Mr. Wonderful, I can head home."

***

"I guess I didn't have to worry about getting involved with anyone unless I take up with a woman. Can you believe it? Everyone here's female." Carrie was complaining already.

"Get a load of the lecturer! No wonder all the ladies turned out," Judy exclaimed. "He's gorgeous!"

"He's probably a pathological liar. Or worse yet, married," Carrie answered.

"He's not wearing a wedding ring."

"I'm not interested."

And true to her word, Carrie just listened. She did not ask questions. She did not laugh at Lecturer Rob's car jokes. They were funny enough; she just wasn't in a laughing mood. Fortunately, she thought, he is wrapping this up pretty quickly. Most of the women started to leave after the talk. They'd quickly determined that there wouldn't be any action in this group and left to go to a singles dance. Judy went to the rest room before heading home.

Carrie sat by herself, watching Rob pack up. She wished Judy had taken her up on her idea of separate cars. Now she had to wait conspicuously by herself for her to finish up in the restroom. She did wonder if Rob was married. He was attractive. Oh, oh, he is coming my way. Carrie's heart started racing, not out of wonderful anticipation, but because she was wondering how she was going to get rid of him. I don't need this. Why me? I was sitting here minding my own business.

"Hi, I'm Rob Stevens, and I just had to ask why you came tonight. You look so bored. I couldn't even get one laugh out of you. Am I a bad story teller?"

"No, your stories were interesting and fun. I guess I'm just in a rotten mood tonight. Actually I found your car tips very helpful." Carrie finally smiled at him, just to be polite.

"Is this a typical singles group meeting? I'm new to the dating scene, and I don't know what to expect."

"Well, fortunately for us gals, there are usually a few men in attendance. The women always outnumber the men, though. It's a shame, because in Sun View there is a fairly even ratio of men to women."

"Have you been maintaining cars all these years and just now getting out from under the hood?" Carrie tried to make a joke.

"No, I'm a widower. Have been for two years but just didn't want to get out. Now I realize that I have to make a new life for myself. Everyone told me I was turning my late wife into a saint. After some counseling, I'm adjusting pretty well," Rob explained.

"I'm sorry I tried to make a joke out of a time that must have been very painful for you," Carrie apologized.

"Well, you can make it up to me by letting me buy you some coffee and explaining the single scene to me. How about it?"

Here I go again. Carrie was trying to think fast about what to do. Rob is very good-looking and nice, but he's already admitted that he thinks of his late wife as a saint. I can never measure up, in his eyes. Don't even want to try, but I feel like I should go with this guy. I don't want to give him too much rejection on his first trip in the singles world.

"Okay, I'll go. Do you want to know where all the singles go after the bars close? You might as well learn the first lesson."

"Where do they go?" Rob was anxious for the lessons to begin.

"Well, I call them the "Second Chance Saloons," but actually it's Denny's or the Belair Diner where everyone goes for a late night snack or early morning breakfast. There'll be lots of singles there, and you can see if any of them look better under fluorescent lights," Carrie said.

Off they went to the Belair Diner where they got a big booth, ahead of the late-night crowd. They opted for coffee and a piece of the specialty of the house, Blueberry Pie. They talked and talked. Carrie always loved being the teacher. She told him all the ins and outs of being single. They laughed a lot as Carrie had a special way of telling a story that made her experiences seem funny.

"So now I've told you everything I know about dating and mating in Sun View. Which one of these beauties do you want to ask out?" By now it was ten p.m., and the crowd was arriving.

Rob glanced all around, pretending to survey the room, and then said very softly with a twinkle in his eye, "I want to ask you out."

Carrie was stunned. She thought of herself as Rob's mentor, not his date. She twisted her napkin around and around in her hand. "You don't want to ask me out. I am much too jaded for a nice guy like you."

"You know, I think, under all that sarcasm and jade, as you call it, there lurks a really nice gal. When you were telling me all about single life in Sun View, I saw glimmers of a sweet, sharp, caring person that I'd like to get to know better."

"I don't know. You said something early tonight that makes me think twice about going out with you. You described your late wife as a saint. I've been there and done that. I dated a guy who just wouldn't let go of his dead wife." Carrie was really nervous. Without thinking, she had torn her straw cover in half and was making a spring out of it, folding the two halves, one over the other. Should I take a chance or is my experience telling me "no," she wondered to herself.

"Look, Carrie, I've been through a lot of counseling. I realize that I have to let go. The counselor even got me to admit in therapy that my late wife was not all that perfect. He explained that I need to move on, and how my wife would have wanted me to date again. The therapist said something that really hit home with me. He said that it would be a great compliment to my late wife if I marry again, that the first marriage was so good I want to try for another successful marriage."

Carrie took his hand in hers and said, "Okay, let's try it. We'll see what happens. I'd better get you out of here before all of these single gals see how good looking you are in the fluorescent light."

***

Much later, Judy asked, "So what happened to Rob?"

"You really want to know?"

"Yes," Judy answered.

"Even though he was a short guy, he had this huge, thick cock, but he rarely wanted to use it. What a waste! He slept a lot. I'd get in bed with him, thinking we were going to have sex. I ended up, watching him sleep. I just got bored with the whole affair. Sorry you asked?"

"No, but I am surprised that would drive you away."

"I'd like to have a love affair that includes sex. Is that asking too much?"

"It might be in this town with lots of older, if not elderly, men."

"I'll keep looking, thank you very much. Someone out there's having fun, even if it's with Viagra."

At home, Carrie got in bed, shooing Charley off the bed. The dog was allowed to sleep on the bed during the day but not with her at night. Why was sex so important to her, she wondered. As she cuddled up, hugging her pillow, she figured out that it was a sign of belonging, the opposite of loneliness which she often felt. She had slept with lots of men and had had lots of sexual experiences. She thought of herself as having quality, not quantity. She wanted a man with whom she could have lazy, comfortable, frequent sex over a long period of time. Not even her two husbands had given her that.

Crazy

"How was your date last night?"

"It was great, Judy. He seems like a nice guy—good job, attractive, available, and attentive. What's there not to like? He's taking me to an inn near Sarasota for dinner this Friday."

"Sounds romantic." Judy always liked romance. She had had little, if any, in her life, Carrie surmised.

***

Friday night arrived. Excited about her date, Carrie was worried, when the phone rang, that it was Ted canceling. It hadn't happened to her very often, but Carrie was a worrier.

"Hello, is this Carrie Bolton?" An unfamiliar female voice was on the other end of the line.

"Yes, who's this?"

"I'm Ted Chastain's wife, and I'm sitting across the street from your house. I'm warning you—you'd better not keep the date you have with Ted." With that, the phone went dead.

What the heck, Carrie wondered to herself. This is weird. Is this lady for real? Could a friend be playing a trick on me? Judy's the only one who knows about the date, and she's not a jokester.

Carrie remembered that she had Ted's cell number. She quickly dialed it. She was in luck. He picked up right away.

"Ted, this is Carrie."

"Hi, Carrie, I'm on my way to your place."

"Ted, I just got a very strange telephone call from a woman who says she's your wife. She says she's sitting across the street."

"Oh God, what did she say?" Ted interrupted.

"She told me that I'd better not keep the date I have with you and then she hung up. I don't know what's going on, but I definitely want to cancel our date."

"Okay. I guess you deserve an explanation. I am married but legally separated. I live in an apartment in my real estate office. She wants me to come back home so she tries to mess up any relationships I start. She is basically harmless. You need a nice, relaxing dinner and some wine tonight to forget the whole episode."

"Well, she didn't sound harmless, and I can't relax now. Maybe another time. After I think my way through this. Sorry! It had sounded like a very pleasant evening." Carrie was shaking now.

"Okay, but I hope you'll let me call you sometime to explain." Ted ended the conversation, realizing that Carrie wasn't in any mood to talk.

A couple of weeks passed, and Carrie thought Ted was out of her life. Carrie was hoping Ted was out of her life. She had dealt with lots of different men and their problems, but she definitely didn't need a crazed wife or ex-wife, whatever she was. It was not to be.

"Hi, Carrie, how've you been?"

"Okay," Carrie said, cautiously.

"Are you calmed down now? I need to talk to you."

"What's there to say? You're married, and I don't want to date you until you're divorced."

"She won't give me a divorce. I've tried everything. Don't I deserve to have a life?"

Ted explained that his wife sits across from his office, watching for him to leave, and then follows him. He explained how he wants to keep in her good graces because she lets him come visit the teenage grandchildren they were raising whenever he wants.

After the call ended, Carrie sat, reflecting on what Ted had said. Should I give him a chance? He was awfully nice.

The phone rang and when Carrie answered, it was Ted's wife. "You're not thinking of dating Ted again, are you?"

"No, I'm not."

"That's good because he's a very sick man. He's been a wonderful father and husband all of his life. When he reached 60, he went off the deep end. He just left us. He wouldn't explain why. He just left."

"There was no reason? He just left? He must have been unhappy," Carrie reasoned.

"No, he was happy."

When Ted called again, Carrie told him what his wife had said. Carrie was searching for answers. He explained that his wife was the one who was sick. She would not let go, that he had been unhappy when he left.

The conversations continued for a couple of weeks. Carrie hated the situation, but she was caught up in it. First, Ted would call and then, shortly thereafter, his wife would call. She thought it was uncanny how his wife would call after he did. Carrie figured that she must have his phones bugged.

One day Carrie just decided to ask. "How do you know to call me right after Ted calls?"

"We have an old business phone in our home, and I can see when he's on the line from the phone buttons."

Carrie was shocked. "Do you mean he's calling from your home?"

"Yes, he's been living here for several months."

Carrie was shocked again. "I thought he lived in the back of his office."

"He did for a while, but I don't think it was really comfortable for him. I asked him to come back, and he did." All of a sudden, she blurted out, "Has he been fucking you?"

"He's tried," was all Carrie said.

"What do you mean 'he tried'?"

"Well, he couldn't get the job done. When he left the bed and didn't come back, I went to check on him. He was in the bathroom, jacking off. I think he's a troubled man."

"He's troubled all right," his wife quickly added.

***

"Yes, I'm back living in my house, but our relationship is very platonic. I sleep on the sofa," Ted explained.

Carrie was half laughing, half-crying. Her nerves were shot. One of these two people is nuts, and I don't know which one it is.

One day, after Ted's wife called, she called a second time, almost immediately after hanging up from the first call. "Listen, Ted was eavesdropping on the other phone when I was talking with you. He's really angry about our conversation. He went down in the basement, got all of his guns, loaded them in the car, and I'm pretty sure he's headed your way. I'd get out of your house, if I were you."

Carrie decided to call the police. When the police arrived and after she had explained the situation, they had Carrie get in the bedroom, and they answered the door. Ted was submissive. He turned over his gun peacefully. "It's time to go back to the hospital, Ted."

Oh, my, what might have happened to me. Carrie was pacing the floor. She was too scared to cry. She felt sick to her stomach. She was sweating profusely. One officer remained behind and tried to calm Carrie. "It's all right; he's a sick man."

Through tears which started to roll down her cheeks, Carrie told how she couldn't tell which of the two was telling the truth in the many telephone conversations she had had with them both.

The officer said, "Don't worry. They're both nuts. They get some kind of thrill out of calling people and scaring them. She's as nuts as he is. They get sexual pleasure out of scaring people, especially women that Ted picks up. She was probably masturbating while she was talking to you. Let me know if she calls again. I think she'll leave you alone now."

After the officer left, Carrie broke down and started sobbing. *What's my life come to? Now I'm attracted to dangerous nut cases. With masturbating wives.* Carrie cried so much she couldn't cry any more. *What am I going to do? I can't stay here. I know they've taken him away but still I'm scared.* Carrie ended up taking her dog and going to Judy's house. She stayed with her a few days. She continued to look over her shoulder often when she was in public. She was worried that, somehow, it wasn't over. Actually she had no more trouble, but it was months before she would answer the phone. She would let it go to the answering machine so she could screen her calls.

I Want to Go with You

"You don't seem to ever have trouble meeting men, right?" Judy was pretty much incredulous at this point by the number of men that had passed through her friend's life.

"Right," Carrie affirmed.

"What's your secret?"

"Well, no secret really. I put men at ease and let them know that I appreciate them in one way or another—maybe by a smile, a compliment, attentive listening, or so on."

"It sure is effective plus you're an attractive lady. That helps too."

"Not really any more attractive than many other women." Carrie was being honest, but she knew she was clever when it came to enhancing what she had.

"Did you ever have men hit on you when you were married?"

"Oh, yes, several. Maybe I'll tell you those stories some day when we are bored in the old-age home," Carrie said, laughing.

That night Carrie had a dream about Kenny and wondered how he was getting along. She kept thinking of him the next day, as she recalled how much he had cared for her.

***

"You're so nice, Kenny, to help me with setting up the desserts," Carrie said.

"My pleasure, ma'am." Kenny was being super polite for a joke. However, Carrie knew that he really was a gentleman, always holding the door for women, getting coffee for his bridge partners, and helping in any way he could.

Every Tuesday night, Carrie brought desserts for the 30-40 people that showed up for duplicate bridge at the bridge center. It was just something she liked to do. She figured even though she wasn't very good at bridge, she could wow them with her delicious concoctions. Kenny was always there bright and early to help her carry them in from the car. Kenny arrived everywhere early. Since his son finally died a few months ago, he really didn't know what to do with himself.

Carrie often checked on him. "How're you doing now, Kenny? Are you able to sleep yet?'

"I can fall asleep, but I wake up every morning about four am and cry. That's still not any better. I guess it'll just take time. Fifteen years is a long time to take care of others with no thought of oneself."

Kenny was an attractive man who belied his 65 years, especially since his hair was light brown. A little Grecian Formula, she suspected. He had been a high school guidance counselor for many years but was now, of course, retired. He spent a lot of time at bridge, playing several times a week. He was very good. Because he was so competent at bridge and because of his wonderful sense of humor, he was a very popular player at all the bridge centers around Indianapolis.

Kenny continued to help Carrie and often sought her out to talk with her before the game started. He gave her many bridge pointers. She noticed at one point that he started touching her arm and hand, something he hadn't done before. Then one evening she swore that he was playing "footsies" with her under the bridge table.

Oh, oh, Carried thought to herself. Am I imagining this or is Kenny starting to make passes at me? He knows I'm married. I must be mistaken.

Carrie started to be on the alert, trying to figure out what was going on. His wife and son have only been dead a few months. Surely he's not getting interested in other women already, she tried to reason.

One night they both arrived very early for the Tuesday night game. As Kenny opened her car door for her, in the twilight, just out of the blue, he leaned down and kissed her. Now she knew.

"Kenny, you can't do that. I'm a married woman. Someone will see you and get the wrong idea."

"You're right; I shouldn't have done that, but I just couldn't help myself.

Don't you have any feelings for me? I thought I detected some little inkling of caring on your part."

"Kenny, I think you're a wonderful man. You're very attractive, intelligent, and funny. If I were available, I would definitely be interested in seeing you more. However, I'm not available. I'm very happily married."

"I'm too old for you, aren't I?"

"No, that's not it at all. I just don't want to get involved with any man outside of my marriage," Carrie patiently explained.

Kenny began to behave, and Carrie and he got along as friends, so she thought. When their favorite game folded and Carrie's partner decided not to play anymore, Carrie was looking for a partner.

"Why don't you play with me? I'll teach you a lot about the game, and you could pick up several master points. You've a lot of potential, but you need to play with one of the better players like me."

Kenny's logic made sense to Carrie. She'd love to play with a good partner and become a much better player. She'd been marking time in bridge for the past couple of years. Because Kenny wasn't making passes at her anymore, she agreed to play with him on Monday nights. In fact, she agreed that he could pick her up at her home and drive her to play every week

They had about a 45-minute ride each way so they did lots of talking. They spent some of the time talking bridge. However, much more of the time was spent getting to know each other. They found out about each other's families, work experiences, marriages, beliefs, and goals. In fact, there was nothing that was off-limits. They had many interesting discussions.

Carrie learned about Kenny's children and the problems he had with them. Mostly, they were always asking for money. He was generous and would often send them large amounts of money. He didn't think it was right. He felt that children should earn their own way, but he could never say "no," and he had it to give.

Carrie learned the terrible ordeal that Kenny went through with his wife and son for the last five years. His wife was a Parkinson's patient and progressively got worse until he had to put her in a nursing home. Right after she died, his son had a debilitating stroke at the young age of forty. For three years he fed him at the facility three times a day and had no other interests in his life. His son finally had a massive stroke and died.

When Carrie and Kenny played bridge, they often did well. "Well, you earned a half a point tonight, Mrs. Bolton. That's real good. You're developing into a really good player. How about stopping for coffee and pie on the way home tonight to celebrate."

"Haven't you had enough pie tonight?" Carrie kidded him.

"Yes, but I want to talk with you, and I know you wouldn't want to pull up alongside the road somewhere to chat or stop for a drink."

Carrie and Kenny stopped at Denny's for coffee. Kenny got right to the point. "We've been playing bridge for almost two years now, but I think I'm going to have to call it quits."

"Kenny, why?" Carrie was puzzled why, out of the blue, he'd want to quit when they were playing so well together.

Kenny continued. "I haven't said anything to you, and I've been a perfect gentleman but being around you is driving me crazy. You see, I'm still in love with you."

"Still in love with me?"

"Yes, I fell in love with you the first time I saw you and talked with you. You're everything I ever wanted in a woman. I know I can't have you but that doesn't stop me from loving you. Your husband is a lucky man." Kenny had tears in his eyes.

"Kenny, I'm so sorry. I didn't know. You're a wonderful man, and you deserve to have a wonderful woman by your side. Unfortunately, it can't be me. But if you look around, there are a lot of nice, unattached ladies to pick from. Think of all the widows that play bridge."

"That's the trouble, as long as I have some connection with you, I don't even notice the other women. That's why I think I want to make a clean break from you. I'll always love you, though."

Carrie and Kenny did stop playing bridge, and Kenny started dating a gal named Elaine. After about six months, Elaine dumped him, and Kenny was devastated.

In the meantime, Carrie and her husband retired to Sun View, Florida, and started a new, active life there. One day, feeling glum, Kenny called Carrie. He told of his failed romance and how depressed he was. Carrie was a little worried that Kenny was going to start to bring up his past feelings for her. He never did. He just sounded like a friend, relating his misfortune. Carrie felt very sorry for him.

"Why don't you come down here for a couple of weeks? Rick and I'd love to see you. We have a big, empty guestroom just waiting for you. And wait until you see all the bridge that's played here. Morning, noon, and night."

Carrie was surprised, but delighted, when Kenny took her up on her offer. Carrie had a plan.

When Kenny arrived, she informed him that she wasn't going to play bridge with him although she played with him a couple of times so he would get to know the various locations where bridge was played.

"Why won't you play with me anymore?"

"Because there are a zillion women down here, many of whom are anxiously seeking men. I want you to go to the games and play. When an attractive lady comes to your table, strike up a conversation. Ask if her husband plays bridge. If she tells you she has no husband and you're attracted to her, ask her for coffee after bridge."

Kenny did just that. After three days, he struck gold. Barbara was a widow, an excellent bridge player—exactly on Kenny's level—and she loved football, another pastime of Kenny's. They hit it off immediately and became inseparable. Kenny began to smile again.

Carrie had big tears of happiness in her eyes as she watched Kenny and Barbara exchange wedding vows, exactly six months after they met. Finally, Kenny was happy again.

Please Don't Talk About Me When I'm Gone

"You're lucky that you never met anyone totally off the wall."

"Oh, I don't know. I thought we agreed that I have had my share of guys with major problems," Carrie answered Judy.

"I'm talking about someone really kinky. A cross dresser, for example."

"I did have a close call one time. Do you want to hear that story?"

"Why not? I've heard all the rest. I might as well have the complete set."

"You definitely have not heard all the rest, but I'll tell you this one quickly. It happened after I moved back to Indianapolis to get away from my memories of Bob, the one into orgies."

***

"What's a single gal like you want with a big, 2800 square foot house?" The realtor actually tried to talk me out of the house and took me, over my protestations, to look at other houses.

"That's the house I want. No need to show me anymore," I explained.

"But that's the first house you looked at!"

"I know, but it's so neat. It has a fireplace, family room with a tile floor, a loft, high ceilings, three bedrooms, and three bathrooms. Builders are just starting to put high ceilings in today's homes, and I want to be in the forefront." I could not be dissuaded.

So I bought the house and started to turn it into my own. I replaced the carpeting and wallpapered some of the rooms. The rest of the rooms needed painting so I went to Sherwin Williams to find a painter. I had used painters they had recommended before and was always pleased.

"Sure, we can help. Call Marge at this number. She's a great painter."

I called Marge. When the telephone was answered, a deep, gruff voice said, "Yeah?"

"May I speak to Marge?"

"This is Marge." The voice was still deep and gruff.

A little wary, I made arrangements for Marge to paint the inside of my home. After all, Sherwin Williams had recommended her.

Marge had a day job and did her painting at night. In my job as engineer for Xerox, I also worked days. I did not have to make special arrangements for Marge to get in to paint. I would be there at night while she painted.

On the appointed day, the doorbell rang. I opened it to find a man standing there. He had short gray hair, stubble on his chin, and was wearing a white tee-shirt and jeans.

All of a sudden, I said to myself, "Wait a minute—those are breasts showing through the tee-shirt!"

Fortunately, Marge identified herself right away so there were no awkward moments although I'm sure I had a strange look on my face.

Marge got right to work. She was a fine painter, very neat if not very fast. As I had newly arrived back in my hometown, I didn't have many nighttime activities yet so Marge and I talked a lot. Maybe that's what took her so long to paint.

We talked about all sorts of things—our history, our families, our dreams, our aspirations, and so forth. She seemed to enjoy talking with me, and I enjoyed talking with her because I found her unusual, not the typical woman, although I am not sure I could have defined what was so unusual about her, once I got past her appearance.

"Well, I'm finally finished," Marge said one day. It had taken her several weeks to finish my house.

"It looks great. I'll certainly recommend you to anyone, if you want me to. But, wow, I'll miss all of our conversations."

"Yes, I will miss you too," Marge said in her usual gruff voice. I had gotten used to her voice and her appearance although, I must say, there were even macho men who were a lot more feminine than she was."

Marge left that night and, sorry to say, I quickly forgot about her, someone who had shared many thoughts and ideas with me.

About six months later I was in Denny's Restaurant. There was Marge, alone in a booth. I went up to her and said, "Hi, Marge."

She said, "Have a seat. It's Mike now."

"Mike?" I was stunned and incredulous.

"Yes, I had both surgeries since I painted for you. The transformation is complete."

Sure enough, her breasts were gone. I can only surmise what the second surgery was.

She…or he was very friendly. All I could think was, I've got to get out of here.

Afraid that he would ask me for a date, I made a quick exit.

***

"Did you like that story, Judy?"

"No. And besides, it doesn't count. You didn't really date him or her or whatever."

It Wasn't God Who Made Honky Tonk Angels

"Let's see, you've dated an alcoholic, a drug addict, an adulterer, a reluctant divorcee, and God only knows what else. Oh, yes, you dated a guy who was into orgies, one who was afraid of commitment, and one who died."

"I didn't realize you're keeping track, Judy," Carrie said.

"It hard not to. Most of these stories are interesting and memorable to me with my boring life."

"If you think about it, you've probably dated some guys who were off the wall too."

Judy responded, "You know I don't date much. I just go to an occasional singles dance here in town. I've just never been swept off my feet by any of the old men around here." Judy was not an especially attractive gal. She was pleasant enough, in a shy sort of way. It didn't surprise Carrie that Judy didn't date much. She should enhance her looks somehow, but that doesn't seem to be her priority. I should help her with makeup, but I don't want to insult her by suggesting it.

"You're right. A lot of the guys around here are old and don't have much of anything left. But every once in a while you run into a gem. You should also check out Tampa and Sarasota for date material."

Judy was still searching for an oddity that Carrie hadn't dated. "I know. You've never dated a guy who you later found out was gay. There's a frontier for you," Judy said, chuckling to herself at her cleverness.

"You're forgetting Marge who turned into Mike. I didn't really date her, I mean him, but I probably could have." Carrie thought back on that lonely time in her life when she had just moved back to Indianapolis. She knew she had spent way too much time talking with a woman who looked like a man. She didn't know too many people, and it was easy to talk with someone painting in her house.

"That doesn't count. I know—you've never dated a guy much younger than yourself."

"Oh yes I have."

"When did that happen?" Carrie had Judy's interest now.

"Well, I'm a little embarrassed to say, but it happened just a few months ago." Carrie made a face as if the whole experience was very distasteful. She had a moment of wistfulness. Malcolm was gorgeous. She was practically licking her lips.

"You never told me."

"You never asked. And I was much too puzzled about the whole thing. It's like he whirled into my life and out again before I knew what hit me. Besides, I feel guilty. Like someone's going to arrest me for child molestation or something."

"How old was he?"

"Thirty-three." Carrie thought about the clear complexion, bright eyes, and fantastic physique. The only thing less than perfect in her young Adonis was his thinning hair.

"Well, that's certainly not a child."

"I know. I was only kidding about the child molestation. But, after all, he is twenty-five years younger than I am."

"That's all the style now—to have a young lover," Judy reminded Carrie. "How did you meet this one?"

"I knew him for about a year before we had our brief affair."

"Yes, go on."

"He was the manager in the local grocery store where I shopped once a week. He was so handsome. I met him first when I had to complain that a cake I had ordered for a meeting of 120 ladies had not been baked. In fact, the clerk did not order the cake from the store's bakery when she was supposed to. I asked to speak to the manager. This gorgeous guy came up and explained how he had just fired the clerk for multiple infractions and how sorry he was that I had no cake. I think I practically drooled when I laid eyes on him. Words wouldn't come out of my mouth.

"And you just let it go at that?"

"Oh, no. He said that the bakery manager would bake me a cake immediately and he would bring it over to the meeting right before the time for it to be served. He got a kick out of my trying to get a lot of freebies out of the deal for my inconvenience. All he would do was give me 50% off of the cake price. I bantered with him to no avail."

"That was the start of a love affair?" Judy didn't get it.

"No, every time I was in the store he would talk to me and kid me about my trying to negotiate a bargain. He was just such a beautiful guy, and I would look forward to our conversations and mild flirting."

"Flirting?"

"Yes, I guess you would call it that. He was always obviously happy to see me. He was sort of a shy guy and did not talk to other customers. At least, I never saw him talking with anyone. He just went about his work. He had this creamy clear complexion, dreamy bedroom eyes, and a fantastic physique. Did I say that before? I was so much in awe that I usually was tongue-tied. Our conversations never lasted long. I've heard older women say, 'Boy, if I were only 20-30 years younger.' Suddenly I knew what they meant. Why, oh why, didn't such a dreamboat come along when I was younger?"

"So when did it become an affair?"

"I was in the strawberry section of the produce department one day, and he came up. I said 'I bet you've come to see what idiot would pay $5.99 for this quart of strawberries.'"

Carrie then started relating the story just as it happened.

The manager said, "Yeah, I have. They're good, though, aren't they? Don't leave the store yet. I have a gift for you." His eye twinkled. Carrie was wondering if this were some sort of joke.

"Wow, a gift for me? Is this part of this store's Christmas spirit—giving regular customers a gift?"

"No, just very special ones. I'll bring it to you after you check out." He gave no more explanation.

Sure enough. There he was at the checkout with a gigantic red poinsettia plant. Carrie thanked him profusely and left the store. A couple of minutes later, there he was at Carrie's car door as she was loading the car and wondering what's going on.

"I have another gift for you, but I want to bring it to your home."

"What am I—the millionth customer or something?"

His eyes were twinkling again. "No, this is for extra special customers. I'll be there in a couple of hours."

Of course, Carrie was flabbergasted. She didn't know what was happening but just decided to go with the flow. She slowly drove home, reliving the whole store scene in her mind. Very slowly, as if in a trance, she unloaded her groceries and her new plant. She didn't want to change into some other clothes because she didn't want to seem too obvious. She did freshen up her makeup, though.

At about four-thirty p.m. he showed up with two bottles of wine. They were cold so he must have had them cooling in one of the store's refrigerated units, Carrie surmised.

Carrie thanked him, put them in the refrigerator, and asked him to sit down in the living room. She was holding one hand in the other because she was so nervous, she was shaking.

"I didn't bring the wine as a gift. I meant for us to drink it now," he said with a devastating smile.

"Oh, okay,' Carrie said. She went back to the kitchen, opened one bottle of wine, and half filled two beautiful crystal wine glasses. They talked for about an hour. He told her all about managing a store and about the people who worked there. He asked her a lot of questions about her life." The wine began to work, and Carrie began to relax. She still didn't understand what was happening, though.

On about the third glass of wine, he moved over to where Carrie was sitting on the sofa and sat down by her but at a comfortable distance. "You're a very lovely lady."

"And you're an extremely handsome young man," Carrie muttered, very embarrassed and at a loss for something to say.

"Let's not talk about age. I think when two people are as attracted to each other as we are, age doesn't really matter, does it?" He was smooth. "Why don't you put on some music?"

"Of course, why didn't I think of that?" Carrie moved across the room and turned the CD player on. As luck would have it, the music was soft mood music. She would have rather put on some Country music, but a lot of people don't like it. And this guy was so smooth, she didn't want him to mistake her for a hillbilly.

When she came back to the sofa, she noticed that he had moved closer to her spot. He set his wine glass down and took one of Carrie's hands in his and kissed the back of it.

This is ridiculous, Carrie thought. He's young enough to be my son. But, somehow, as he continued to kiss her hand and then put his arm around her, his age suddenly didn't matter to her either.

As the music played and the room darkened after the sunset, they began to caress and kiss. This is crazy but wonderful, Carrie thought. Her animal instincts started to take over. She wanted him. I want to possess him and be possessed by him. I want him on me and in me.

Slowly he began to take off the tie and starched white shirt he always wore to work. His very broad shoulders turned Carrie on even further. Just as in the store, his motions were slow and measured. Therefore, it didn't surprise Carrie that he very leisurely lowered and folded his pants. His bikini briefs revealed a big hard-on. Carefully and deliberately he lifted Carrie's skirt and slid his hand to her pussy. She let out a low moan as he massaged her. A slow smile came over his face. Knowing that she was ready, he started making love to her on the sofa. Their passion was such that the first round was over pretty quickly.

When he started a second time, Carrie suggested the bed. My old bones don't like the contortions I have to go through in the living room. She was amazed that he could make love a second time so soon after the first but reminded herself that he was young. This time he made slow, leisurely love. After they were finished, they slept for a few minutes.

"I have to go now, but I would like to come over next week on Wednesday about the same time. Would that be okay?"

Carrie was still reeling from her orgasms and would have agreed to about anything. When he left, she sat, staring off into space. What just happened? I can't believe it. I can't even tell anyone. They won't believe a young man, practically a kid, would be interested in me enough to make love to me. Twice, no less.

***

"And that's the story of my young boyfriend, Judy."

"Gosh, I'm panting. Did he come back?" Judy was fascinated by the story.

"Oh, yes. For about two months, every week, we visited and then made love. The sex got better and better until it was pretty fantastic."

"Which store does this dreamboat manage?" Judy was curious.

"Oh, no, you don't. I'm not saying. He's still in town and managing the store." Carrie was afraid the story would get out although she was sure she wasn't the first, nor would she be the last of his customer conquests.

"What do you know about him? Is he married?"

"I never asked, and he never said. I imagine he is."

"Did he just get tired of the whole thing and stop coming over?"

"No, I did. At first the attentions of a young man were flattering. It was fun and exciting. However, after a while I realized that this was not in line with my goals. I wanted to go out and have fun with other people. I wanted to dance and dine out and go on trips. I didn't want to be a back street woman."

"Did you tell him this?"

"No, I told him that I had met and wanted to date someone else." Carrie remembered that she wanted no arguments from him. She figured if she told him anything else, he would have an answer for it. This way he could think that he had been replaced in her affections.

Carrie continued, "He accepted it as if he knew that this was the way the affair would end. He seemed to sense that what he had to offer was not enough. I don't think he could offer more. He told me that I was a wonderful lady and that he would always have a special place in his heart for me. And...somehow...I believed him."

After Judy left, Carrie was still thinking about her young lover. I could use his attention about now. Actually she was smiling, not at her horniness, but at the way she had handled the episode. She was puffed-up proud she could make a decision that was good for her and her goals. She did miss him, though.

Making Believe

"You had two marriages which were not ideal. Did you ever step out on your husbands?" Judy had poured herself a second cup of coffee while Carrie loaded the dishwasher.

"No, Judy, never."

"Weren't you tempted? I mean you weren't bouncing on the love trampoline at home with your first husband."

"No, I never had an affair."

"Never? Nothing?"

"You're getting awfully nosy," Carrie said with a smile. "But if you must know, I discovered the fine art of flirtation. That kept me amused."

"What the heck is that?"

"Let me describe a flirtation I had recently and then you'll understand."

"First, there was Joe. When I saw him sitting at the end of the table at a sorority social, I thought he was the handsomest man I had seen in a while."

"And..."

"You know Sun View is really a very small community, about 20,000, and there are all sorts of meetings, concerts, shows, and parties. I knew I would run into him again. I had a plan and would just wait for my opportunity. Sure enough, the next time I saw him was at a community meeting with about 900 residents in attendance. I saw him about sixty feet away, across the crowded room. However, he was not so far away that I couldn't stare at him while I was talking to another person. I stared at him for a long time. Finally, he noticed. I kept staring. After he noticed me, he kept looking at me to see if I was still staring."

"That's weird, Carrie. Almost demented."

"But it works."

"What do you mean it works?"

"The next time I saw him, he was very friendly to me and, of course, I reciprocated."

"Then what happened?"

"Well, I spent a lot of time fantasizing what it would be like to have an affair with him—where we would meet, what would be said, what would happen, what screwing him would be like, and so on."

"All of that and yet you had no affair?"

"No affair. However, I overheard him tell a friend he found me very attractive so I knew I had got to him. I started to give him sly looks with sly smiles, and he came back by winking at me with his own sly smile. I remember a presentation he gave to about a hundred people. He addressed all of his comments to me."

"What?"

"He looked constantly at me for most of the presentation, as if I were the only person in the room. I saw several people look at me. I'm sure they were wondering what was going on."

"This is all very bizarre, Carrie."

"I know, but these flirtations make me feel good about myself, that I can still get a man interested in me, even if from afar. When your husband is not screwing you, as my first wasn't, you start to have bad feelings about yourself, that you're not attractive any more. Really, the flirtations gave me something to look forward to."

Carrie continued, "These flirtations went on for so long Joe and I actually felt very close to each other. When we talked, we enjoyed each other so much we had a difficult time stopping the conversation."

"What stopped you?"

"His wife would walk up or my husband would come around or the meeting would start or whatever."

"And there was never anything physical?"

"Oh, while talking with me, he would rub my arm or grab my hand for a second. When greeting me at a meeting, for example, he would hug me and sometimes kiss me but that was it. There was definitely chemistry happening, though."

"That would drive me wild," Judy panted.

"Sometimes it definitely did. But I knew I didn't want a sexual relationship."

"Wow!"

"I know, strange. But, you know, I think it made me a better wife. I didn't feel unfulfilled anymore, and maybe out of guilt, I treated my husband better and he, in turn, treated me better."

"Did these flirtations ever backfire?"

"Yes—once—almost."

"What happened?" Judy just could not believe this conversation.

"It was when I was working. I had to work for a short period of time with a guy named Jon. He was so cute in looks and manner. I was instantly attracted to him."

"Did you stare at him?"

"Not at first. I had to get his attention first, which I did by asking a lot of questions about him and his life under the guise of small talk. In other words, I showed him a lot of attention and complimented him a lot."

"When did the staring start?"

"After three or four weeks. I started the staring, and he picked up on it right away, giving me soulful looks from across the room. At parties we would spend a lot of time together, talking and flirting. Sparks would fly, the chemistry was that electric."

"So when did you get in trouble with this flirtation?"

"After three or four months of flirting, I realized I definitely wanted to have an affair with him. Fortunately for me, he seemed quite content just to flirt."

"Did you come out of the closet, so to speak, to him and reveal your desire for an affair?"

"I came really close to doing that a few times, but something would always stop me. I finally realized that he was not going to start an affair with me, and I didn't want to be the one to start it. I don't know if I could have if I had really wanted to."

"So how did it all end?"

"It took me forever to get out of the flirtation and the desire to have an affair. I would take long walks. I would pray. I even went to a counselor. She helped a lot although, for the life of me, I can't remember what she said that helped so much."

"That was a close call."

"Yeah, it was. I really think my prayers are what helped the most. I prayed, "Dear God, please remove him from my life or please remove my love for him." After a couple of months, he was transferred out of my office and was never around me any more."

Carrie continued, "From that experience, I learned a lot. I learned not to get too carried away. I've never made that mistake again. I now know it's just a flirtation. I've learned it's better to have flirtations with several men at the same time. That keeps me from getting too intense with any one man. You know, safety in numbers."

"When you write your memoirs, I wonder what you will entitle this chapter."

"How about 'So Many Men, So Little Time?'"

Danny Boy

"You've had a lot of sex in your life," Judy said out of the blue one day.

"That's a strange comment from out of nowhere but yes and no, I've had sex with a lot of different men, but I've not ever had sex on a real regular basis. There was the four and a half year relationship with Bob. That was the longest time. Other times I went long periods with no sex."

"Having sex with so many different men—didn't you worry that you would get a disease?"

"Yes, I did, but I was very careful. First of all, I didn't go out with sleezeballs. The men I dated didn't sleep with lots of different women. Secondly, the diseases were not so prominent then. No one had heard much of Herpes, for example. And also, I was very careful and lucky, I suppose."

"That's good. You'd better be careful now, though. There's disease everywhere, even here in Sun View.

"That's what I hear." Returning to the previous subject, Carrie said, "Actually what I worried about the most was getting pregnant."

"That would have been a worry. You're lucky that it never happened to you."

Carrie paused for the longest time. Should she tell her the story? Could Judy handle it?

"Judy, there's a story that I've wanted to tell you for a long time. Actually, you know most of the story, but you don't know all of it." Carrie had kept it from her friend for many years.

"What is it?"

"It happened a long time ago when I was married to Bill," Carrie said as she began daydreaming about a very sad episode in her life. She began to relate the story to Judy.

***

“Sally wants to come visit”, Carrie told her husband, Bill. “I wonder what’s up. She never visits me.” Sally liked Carrie, loved her in fact, but she never wandered far from home. Always, Carrie was the one who had to visit at her house.

Sally is the oldest daughter of her dearest friend, Judy. Judy and Carrie and Judy’s cousin, Kathy, have a friendship that goes back to the third grade. They were all members of the Blue Bird Club. Carrie didn’t realize how strong their friendship was until the day she got kicked out of the club for running around the furnace during a club meeting. Judy and Kathy both stood up and said, “If Carrie goes, we go,” and marched out of the room, the house, and the club forever.

Judy and Carrie became almost inseparable. They had sleepovers at Judy’s house but never at Carrie’s. Judy tried sleeping at Carrie’s house once but had to have her father come get her in the middle of the night. Carrie even slept with her in the same bed when she missed a semester due to a diagnosis of mononucleosis. They double-dated. They told each other every secret they had. They worked at the same little grocery store. They vacationed together at Judy’s parents’ cottage on the Upper Peninsula of Michigan. They were definitely closer than many sisters.

So when Sally wanted to visit, Carrie immediately agreed and waited apprehensively for her visit. In just a short time, Sally and her boyfriend arrived. Now Carrie really knew something was wrong! Sally was never on time. In fact, no one in Sally’s family was ever on time. Carrie was convinced that it was something in their genes.

Sally and Mike came into the room. Sitting in the family room, they crowded together, practically on the same cushion, on her big sofa. Carrie can remember about 30 seconds of small talk, when the conversation stopped, and Sally announced in a soft voice, “I’m pregnant”.

Carrie was shocked!

Many girls get pregnant out of wedlock, but Carrie had never dreamed it would happen to Sally. Sally was a shy gal and very sweet. All of Judy’s kids were shy, maybe not at home, but definitely in public. None had dated very much. Immaculate Conception even crossed Carrie’s mind!

Sally asked her for money for an abortion. Judy had worked hard during high school. Because of this, she had never wanted any of her kids to work to allow plenty of time for childhood fun so it was not a surprise that this recent high school graduate didn't have any money.

Carrie was not in favor of loaning or giving anyone money. She had never borrowed or asked for money, and she didn't think others should either. Anyway, Carrie said, "Sally, your mother will give you any money you need."

Sally, in tears at this point, said, "My mother will kill me for getting pregnant; I can't ask her; I can't even tell her anything about this."

"Your mother will rant and rave for about a week, and then she will be okay with it," Carrie explained. "Your mother loves kids and, eventually, she will be thrilled that there is going to be another baby in the family."

Sally was not convinced, but Carrie knew it was true. Judy did love kids. She was a very wonderful kindergarten teacher, the kind every parent would want for his or her child—lovingly strict, fair, attentive, imaginative, playful, and dedicated to the teaching profession.

Sally went on. "No, I want an abortion. I've thought a lot about it, and I can't have a baby now. Mike and I aren't married, we have no money, and we both live at home."

"You know that there is never a convenient time to have a baby, don't you, Sally?" Carrie explained that there would never be enough money for a baby or enough time for a baby. Carrie pointed out that babies often interrupt educations, careers, good marriages, bad marriages, and ended by explaining how their lives will always be filled with activities that will have to be interrupted to have a baby. "Sally and Mike, you don't want to kill your baby just because it's not convenient to have him or her now."

Sally thought this over and began to cry again. "What will my mother think? What will my friends think?"

"Sally, the important thing is what you will think. Do you want to wake up at night for the rest of your life, sweating from a bad dream about your aborted child, wondering if you had gotten rid of a boy or a girl? Do you want to admire every child you see and then wonder what your child would have been like? Do you want to cry every year on the anniversary of the abortion? Do you want to always know, regardless of how good a life you try to lead, that you committed a terrible sin in your early life? Sally, this is a serious, life-altering decision."

Sally and Mike left. Carrie worried that she had not said the right things. She had wanted to be supportive, but Carrie definitely did not want her to abort the child. She knew screaming "don't do it" at the top of her lungs would not have helped.

Carrie didn't hear anything for a couple of weeks. Finally, Sally called and said, "I thought about what you said, and I'm not going to have an abortion." ("Thank, God", Carrie thought.) "I want you to tell my mom, though; I just can't do it. You can tell her some of the things you told me."

Carrie scheduled a quiet lunch with Judy in their favorite restaurant. They were close friends so Carrie did not have to beat around the bush. "Judy, Sally is going to have a baby." There were no tears, no rantings, and no ravings. Judy just smiled and quietly said, "She is? Is she sure?"

Six months later, on September 22, a lovely baby girl was born and named Briana. There were lots of tears—Judy's, Sally's, and Carrie's—when Sally asked Carrie to be Briana's godmother.

***

"If you had only known, the total irony of it all, Judy! Briana, you see, was born on the exact date, September 22, of my abortion several years before. Every day I wish I had sought the counsel of a friend back then because—to this day, my nightmare has never ended!"

Judy hugged Carrie and held her for the longest time while they both cried softly. After her friend left, Carrie cursed the doctor again for telling her the aborted child was male. Since then Carrie thinks often of her dead son. She thinks of him every September 22 and calculates how old he would be if he had lived. She wonders what her son would have been like.

She named him Danny, a favorite name of hers. Whenever she hears the song "Danny Boy", she dissolves into tears and has to excuse herself. There are many theories about what the songwriter had in mind when he wrote "Danny Boy", but Carrie prefers to think it's a mother's song to her son who has gone away but who will be reunited with her in the afterlife.

Two Lips, Two Arms, Too Lonely, Too Long

"I do not believe it!" Carrie couldn't decide if what she saw and overheard at the funeral was outrageous or hilarious. She'd just returned from the service for the wife of a good friend and associate in a Sun View club. In fact, she stopped by Judy's house to tell her about the incident.

"What don't you believe?" Judy poured her friend a glass of wine to calm her down.

"Well, it's not exactly my business, but it seemed in such poor taste. Poor Paul is so devastated at the loss of his wife. He cried as he visited with each person after the service. I was wandering through the large crowd and came close to him when I overheard a gal introducing another woman to Paul. Her next sentences after the introductions were 'Maybe you two could start dating. You're going to be very lonely. Maggie here is a recent widow and is lonely too.' Can you believe it? Poor Janice is not even cold in the ground yet and this broad is trying to set Paul up."

"My gosh. I've heard of the casserole brigade, but this is ridiculous. Don't look so quizzical, Carrie. You know as soon as there's an available man, the ladies start going after him with their wonderful home cooking and their other wares. What did Paul do when this gal tried to fix him up?"

"He was obviously embarrassed and at a loss for words. Finally, he mentioned that maybe they could get together sometime." Carrie was lost in another world for a minute as she thought about Paul. He is a good-looking guy. I've often thought of flirting with him but can't bring myself to do it as he's such a nice man and is always telling me what a nice person I am. Little does he know.

"Do you think I'm perceived as a nice person, Judy?"

"Heavens, yes! Why do you ask such a question?"

"Oh, I don't know. I've a pretty checkered past. I don't always use the nicest language. In fact, a lot of the time it sounds pretty tough. I dress like trailer trash."

"Yes, but most people don't know about your past. Most think of you as a tireless volunteer, who is very kind and service-oriented. I feel you 'think' tough, but speak in a very refined way in public. And, please, you don't dress like trailer trash. While you have a certain sex appeal in the way you dress, you are usually in very classic, tailored clothes." Judy didn't understand the reason for this question but tried to answer it as honestly as possible.

"I think Paul will survive. He's a very smart man and will get help if he needs it. Besides, there's always Maggie, the wannabe date," Carrie said, laughing. Judy was chuckling too.

***

"Gee, Paul, I'm really glad to see you back at our club meetings. Did you go back home to visit with family?" Carrie was really happy to see him after a month's absence.

"No, I needed to take a little time for myself. To sort things out, literally and figuratively. There's a lot of paperwork to deal with after a spouse dies." At that point another club member came up and welcomed Paul back. Carrie bowed out of the conversation.

Carrie went ahead and found a seat for herself. The weekly meeting was about to start. The only thing she doesn't particularly care for about the meeting is that it's exactly one hour long. During that hour there isn't time to talk with table companions—the meal is served and consumed while the program speakers address the group.

Afterwards, as she was about to get into her car, Paul came rushing up. "Do you have time to get some coffee? I want to talk with you."

"Sure. Your car or mine? Or do you want me to follow you somewhere?" Carrie assumed Paul wanted to talk about a community service project which they had been planning together.

They sat opposite each other in a booth at the new Bob Evans restaurant and ordered coffee. Talk quickly turned to various club projects including the one for community service. Paul talked at length of his plans for another project involving at-risk kids which he would like Carrie's help with.

"I'll help you with anything, Paul. You know that."

"Yes, you are a very helpful and nice person, Carrie. Have I told you that before?" A slow smile crossed Paul's face. He seemed very nervous, though.

"Paul, you're always telling me that." Carrie was amused.

"I tell you because I don't know how else to tell you I like you. In fact, I didn't bring you here to talk club business, but to tell you I want to date you."

As Carrie started to speak, Paul interrupted and said, "But I can't. It's too soon. It's only been a month since Janice's death. I'm still going through some hard times. But I wanted you to know I care for you very much."

Carrie wasn't sure what to say. "I think you're a wonderful man, and I would be honored to date you when the time's right."

"I think I should wait at least six months. Don't you agree? I don't want people talking. I loved and respected my wife. I don't want people thinking otherwise."

"Whatever seems right for you will be okay with me." Paul looked so adorable Carrie wanted to grab and kiss him.

"Maybe I could call you once in a while, though. No one would have to know." Paul asked Carrie if his call would be okay.

Carrie quickly agreed, and they drove back to where Carrie's car was parked. The parking lot was empty now.

"May I seal our agreement with a kiss?" Paul didn't have to wait for an answer. Carrie moved closer. Taking her head in his hands, Paul gave Carrie a tender kiss. As he moved away, Carrie's eyes twinkled and she said, "I want another one, please." This time they kissed with passion.

***

Carrie couldn't get Paul out of her mind. She thought about him day and night. *Why hasn't he called? I could definitely feel the heat and the chemistry during our kiss. I didn't think he would wait this long to call.*

Carrie went about her daily routine half-heartedly. She guessed she would have to wait the six months even to hear from Paul. She didn't understand how she could miss him so much as he hadn't even been in her life, other than as a friend, just a short two weeks ago.

One night around ten o'clock, after about three weeks had passed since their two brief kisses, the telephone rang. It was Paul. "I just couldn't wait any longer to talk with you. Lord knows I tried. How have you been? I've really missed you."

"I've missed you too," Carrie said. "I think something wonderfully good started with that kiss of ours. I'd like to be holding you in my arms now."

"Oh, yes, I'd be kissing your neck, blowing in your ear, and nibbling on your earlobe."

"Paul, you devil!"

"I can't help myself. I'm so attracted to you. How I'm going to be able to wait four months, I'll never know. But I've got to do it. The ladies have been calling to inquire about how I'm getting along. I've had several invitations for home-cooked meals. I turn them all down, though. If I go anywhere, it'll be to your house."

"You have a standing invitation."

"I could slip over there right now. Are you ready for bed?"

"Yes, I have my nightgown on, and I was reading in bed."

"What's your nightgown like? Is it one of those little, skimpy teddies?"

"Paul, really!. I think you're horny."

"You better believe I am. I have a great big stiff cock right now. I shouldn't' have said that. Does that bother you, Carrie?"

"I'm just a little surprised. You are always so controlled, so refined, at club meetings."

"Of course! But I do have a sexual side too."

Carrie's pussy was getting moist and was getting in the swing of things. "What would you like to do with that great big stiff cock?"

Paul moaned. "First of all, I would guide your head to it, hoping you would lick it and then suck it a little to get it going."

"I'd love to suck your cock. I could suck it all evening. That really turns me on. But I don't want to do it too long, as I don't want you to climax. I want to feel you inside of me. I love that too."

"Baby, I could make love to you all evening. I'd start by sucking those big titties of yours. Then I would slowly move down your body, licking all the way. I have a long cock and a long tongue. I'd use my tongue to make your clit twitch and beg for more."

"Oh, my God. I'm about ready to come."

Paul shouted, "Don't come yet. I've only just begun. I'm stroking my cock, pretending it's in your tight little cunt. Oh, I want you. I know it will be fantastic."

Carrie had gotten out her vibrator and was massaging her clitoris as Paul talked. With his talk, she was hardly able to keep from coming. "I want you to stick it in me. Please, Paul, fuck me, fuck me. Oh, please fuck me."

"I'll fuck you all right, but first I want to glide it in and start slowly. Just a slow in and out until you're begging for more."

"Oh, I would be begging," Carrie said, letting out a low, guttural sound.

"After I get you good and lathered up, I would start pumping a little faster. Faster and faster until I'm really banging you good."

"I love it hard. Give it to me hard. I want you to fuck me hard. Please come over and fuck me, Paul. I need it so bad. How much dick do you have to give me?"

"I have a big, thick eight inches, just pulsating in my hand. I'm getting ready to come, Carrie. Are you ready? I'm sorry I'm so fast this time."

"Don't worry. I've been ready for some time. Here I come. Omigod! Yes, it's good; it's the best. Don't ever leave me, Paul. I need you; I need your cock." Carrie was screaming in ecstasy. She didn't hear Paul was screaming too.

When they both recovered, Paul said, "Wow, we're both screamers. We will rock the house when we finally get together."

Carrie laughed and asked, "Did we just have phone sex?"

"I think so. I've read about it but have never done it. My wife wouldn't have gone for anything like that. I hope you're okay with everything. I don't want to drive you away. I'm just so turned on by you."

"I'm okay. It was fun. Not as good as the real thing, but still satisfying. I'm really turned on by you too." Carrie was sweating and thinking of another shower she needed to take.

"I think you'll be able to sleep now. Sweet dreams. I'm going to hang up now. I'll call you soon, my darling."

***

A couple of days later Paul called, and they had phone sex again. This time it took longer. They weren't as sex-starved as the first time. In fact, every couple of days Paul called Carrie and, after they caught up on the day's events, they would start romancing over the wire. They were both enjoying their physical relationship, albeit a long-distance one.

Their telephone romance went on for a couple of months then Paul started calling less frequently. Carrie began to worry. She had thought they were getting closer. When she didn't hear from him for a week and a half, Carrie broke her promise to herself and called him.

"I've been missing you. Why haven't you called, Paul?"

"Carrie, I don't know how to tell you this, but I've met someone else whom I want to date."

Carrie was devastated and could hardly choke back her sobs. "I thought we were going to get together soon. How could you have met someone else? You haven't been dating, have you?"

"No, Carrie, I didn't lie to you. I haven't been dating anyone and haven't been having phone sex with anyone but you. I met this gal in my grief counseling seminar. She's a really nice gal like you, and I want to take her out."

"So, we're just over, finished? I thought you cared for me, other than for sex. I feel cheated, Paul."

"You have every right to hate me, Carrie. I didn't mean to lead you on. I really thought we would get together, but I feel now there's too much water over the dam, if you know what I mean."

"Okay, have a great life, Paul," Carrie said as she slammed down the receiver. I'll never participate in phone sex again. I would have liked to have seen his eight inch cock, though, if he had one. He's probably really a pencil dick. Carrie reached for her vibrator.

I Always Get Lucky with You

It was a rainy day in usually sunny Florida. Judy had nothing to do. She put the plastic flaps down on her golf cart and drove over to Carrie's house.

As Judy sat down in her favorite chair at the kitchen table, Carrie asked "Do you want some coffee or do you want some of the soup I made today?" Earlier Carrie had whipped up some soup because she thought it sounded good on this rainy day although it wasn't cold out.

"I'd rather have some scotch."

"Scotch? I've never known you to drink scotch," Carrie continued, "but you're in luck. Rick always drank scotch, and I have some of his left. I never touch the stuff. It tastes like poison to me."

"Well, I'll drink it in his memory. Speaking of your late husband, how'd you meet Rick?" Judy thought today seemed like a good day for one of Carrie's stories.

"I advertised in the paper for him."

"What? In the classifieds?"

"No. There was a service called Dateline or something like that. I actually tried dating via the personal ads a couple of times in my life. Once was right after my divorce. I enjoyed having personal ad dates at that time but actually found my next romance at the bridge table after about a year. That relationship with Charles, my bridge partner, lasted two and a half years until I knew I had to get out of it. However, Charles and I had such a nice social life that I was having trouble breaking up with him. I decided to put an ad in the paper to see if I could find someone so appealing that Charles wouldn't matter to me anymore."

"What did you say in your ad?"

"Basically my ad said I was looking for a guy who was retired and wanted to spend part of the year in Florida and part in Indianapolis. The ad attracted fifteen guys. Most of them sounded like potential dates. However, unfortunately, I got sick after calling and listing all the guys' names and telephone numbers. The doctors could not figure out what was wrong with me. I was miserable and in a lot of pain. The sickness dragged on for three months. I was sure I was dying. I went out and bought a recliner so that I would have something comfortable in which to spend my last days."

"You're so funny, Carrie. That sounds like you. So you must have gotten back to your list eventually—you're not dead, and you met Rick, your second husband."

"Fortunately, the doctors finally diagnosed my problem, which was, for all its pain, a rather minor condition. Proper medicine put me back in a man-shopping mood. I started down my list of men. Most of them were no longer interested because they had found someone to date."

Carrie continued, "One guy was still out there looking on my second go-round. He had seemed so interested in me on our first date but then turned me down cold when I used the old "I have two tickets" trick. I reminded him, the second time, that I apparently wasn't the one for him.

"I called another guy named Rick. He had a very deep, resonant voice and sounded like a radio announcer. He was articulate and interesting. My first reaction was to wonder what was wrong with him. We talked for hours. After being reasonably sure that he was not married, which was a constant worry on the personal ad circuit, I agreed to meet him at the Steak and Ale Restaurant for a drink."

"Did you hit it off right away?" Judy wondered.

"I walked into the restaurant and saw this attractive guy sitting at the bar. I wondered where my date was then I realized that the attractive guy was my date. Okay, so far, so good. We talked again for about an hour. He seemed very nice and told me of two long-term failed marriages, so his armor did have a chink. However he won me back when he told me how he was going to wait until he found a lady that really loved him this time. He seemed very interested in me, but I was tired and left, against his wishes, after about an hour. He said he would call."

"'Has he called yet,' my Mother kept asking me, for the third week in a row."

"No, and you might as well stop asking me. He's not going to call. He's just another weirdo." I answered Mom as I was fuming inside. Why had he bothered to act so interested if he wasn't going to call? I just didn't get it but resigned myself to 'anything goes' in the world of personal ad dating."

When I arrived home from work one Friday, the telephone was ringing. It was Rick. He started talking as if no time had passed. I wanted to say, 'Where the hell have you been?' but managed something more ladylike."

"So what was his excuse for waiting three weeks to call?" Judy asked.

"He explained that he had to get rid of his current girlfriend."

"So he hadn't been so lonely after all!"

Carrie continued, "He explained that there is a right way and a wrong way to dump someone. I just hope no one ever takes three weeks to dump me. Just get it over with quickly, I say."

"Anyway, Rick became my husband. Yes, my newspaper romance had a happy ending. We got a big kick out of telling people of our meeting through an ad. Rick loved to say that he answered my ad just to see what a swinging single ninety-year-old lady would be like. He said my ad made me sound quite old. I would remind him of how close he came to being racked up as just one more flake!"

"Well, what did you like about Rick?" Judy still hadn't really heard a description of love at first sight or fireworks or chemistry.

"Well, for starters, he was very well endowed," Carrie said, smiling a sly grin.

"It always gets back to that, does it? You seem to be obsessed with a man's genital size," Judy complained.

"I'm not obsessed, but sex is important to me. It's one of the fun parts of life. And if I'm going to have sex, especially on an extended basis, such as in marriage, I want it to be good."

"And size makes it good?" Judy asked.

"Well, that's not the only thing, but that's important to me. It's a very erotic thought. I've had outstanding sex with small, medium, and large, but large and thick is best. Now I'm not saying I like gigantic. In fact, anything over eight inches gives me gas."

"What?" Judy couldn't believe her ears.

"Yes, gas. A really long one goes in so far that I guess it pushes against my colon wall and gives me gas. There I am—screwing and farting, screwing and farting."

"Oh, thanks for that image," Judy said, laughing. "Seriously, what was the attraction?"

"He was breathing," Carrie joked. "No, seriously, he was attractive, very intelligent, very well-traveled, educated, very active, a take-charge type, and—well-endowed."

"Okay, I get the picture. Sex was a very big part of your life with Rick, right?" Judy asked.

"It was at first. After we got married, we were very active people in all aspects of life, including sex. But then, just a couple of years after we were married, Rick had a stroke."

"That ended it then, huh?"

"That ended a whole lot of things, but it didn't end sex totally. We still had a sex life clear up until his death, but not as frequently as before. It also changed the nature of it—the missionary position was out of the question. We had to be very inventive."

"Rick's stroke must have been terrible on both of you," Judy sympathized.

"It was, at least at first. It was the end of a lot of dreams we had for the two of us. I had such a terrible time of it that I finally had to go to a counselor and get help. I just couldn't understand why I resented Rick. He was the one who was sick, not me. It wasn't his fault he had the stroke. The counselor was very helpful. She explained that a stroke is a family affair. It affects everyone. She helped me to cope with it, psychologically anyway. I still had a lot to learn about being a caregiver 24 hours a day, though."

"Rick required lots of help?" Judy hadn't heard about all of this before. Carrie kept her second marriage to herself. Now that she was talking, Judy wanted to hear it all.

"Yes, and at first, it was overwhelming. I had to do everything—cooking, cleaning, yard work, driving, paying bills, and waiting on him, hand and foot. He needed help with everything—showering, dressing, eating, walking to his wheelchair, etc."

"I can see why you were resentful," Judy added.

"Whoa, I was only resentful right at first. I realized that this was now going to be my life, and I had to make the best of it or I was going to be miserable always. Besides, Rick started to improve ever so slightly. I have always been angry with the doctors because they told us Rick would never get better. Well, over the next couple of years, he did get better. He got so he could dress himself (except for his shoes and socks) and eat without help. We bought an electric cart which helped a lot. No more pushing or lifting a heavy wheelchair. Most importantly, I learned to cope. I learned all the new skills I needed. I got so I could do them by rote."

"My gosh, you sacrificed a lot," Judy commented.

"At first I did, but eventually Rick and I learned to manage. I got to the point where I could get him set up at home and then go out and do my thing—you know, volunteer in clubs, go to concerts, etc. Rick had a wonderful attitude. He wanted me to have a life away from him. He encouraged me to go and have fun. In that way, he was a saint."

"That was very generous of him. Many men in his condition would have complained and wanted your undivided attention."

"I know. It could have been a whole lot worse. Rick was very unusual in that he didn't complain, had a wonderful attitude, and was sure he was going to be healed tomorrow." Carrie got teary-eyed, thinking of Rick's generous and optimistic spirit.

Carrie continued, "Rick had done it all in his earlier years. That's one of the reasons he was so content in his sickness. He had traveled all over the world, flown airplanes, skydived, raced Porsches, entertained extensively, all the while working in three wives, one by one, of course, and raising two sons. He was a traveling salesman and all the stories you hear about them were true in Rick's case. He romanced hundreds of women, all over the world. We used to compare notes and laugh at each other's escapades. He certainly didn't miss much in life."

"How'd it all end?" Judy had to go but wanted to hear the end of this love story.

"Rick developed congestive heart failure. One day his heart just couldn't take any more, and he had a massive heart attack. I was devastated, on a lot of levels. I loved Rick, of course, but also his care was a large part of my life. I was lost with very little to do, no one to take care of. Rick and I had grown very close, fighting his illnesses together. I was lost without his companionship. I'm sure that's hard to understand, Judy."

"You forget that I'm a widow too and took care of Richard in his final days," Judy reminded Carrie.

"Although I've been single a lot, I think my good relationship with Rick, despite his illness, is the reason I am so lonely now. I want that closeness again."

"That's a nice tribute to Rick—that you want to get married again." Judy tried to console her friend, who had started crying softly.

Every Day I Have to Cry Some

"What's wrong? You look very upset." Judy had never seen her friend look as if all the color had drained out of her face. Carrie was as pale as a ghost.

"That was my friend Annie. She wants to come over. She has something to tell me, and she doesn't want to do it on the phone," Carrie replied.

"That sounds interesting."

"I don't think so. Annie was crying—sobbing, in fact."

"Has she been well? Could she have some dread disease?" Judy tried to solve the puzzle.

"Oh, I hope not. That's what I'm worried about, but she's been fine, as far as I know."

Carried tried to explain Annie to Judy, "While you are my best friend, Annie is a close second. We met while we both were officers in the Garden Club. At 70 years old, Annie is a lovely woman, a former beauty queen, in fact. She and her husband Edward have a beautiful home on Granger Drive and really don't want for any material things in life. Annie and Edward raised four children and are a loving couple. They love to dance and are quite good at it."

"Gee, I hope there's not trouble in paradise," Judy offered.

"No, their marriage is rock solid. They hold hands a lot, and Edward buys all sorts of beautiful jewelry for Annie on special occasions and also for no reason at all. In fact, they're getting ready to celebrate their fiftieth wedding anniversary next year."

Judy grabbed her handbag and started to leave. "I'm getting out of here so Annie won't hesitate to talk." Judy opened the backdoor and exited through Carrie's garage, practically running to her car. "Be sure to call me," she shouted as she opened the car door.

***

"Come in, Annie. You've had me on pins and needles, wondering what's wrong."

Annie looked bad. Usually impeccably dressed and made up, she had no makeup on and had been crying for a long time from the looks of her hollowed, red-rimmed eyes.

"Edward had an affair."

"What! Not Edward! Are you sure?" Carrie was shocked.

"Yes, I saw an email message she wrote him, professing undying love and revealing details of their intimacy. She even said that her pussy ached for him. Gross!"

"Oh, my God. This is dreadful. What did you do?"

"I went wild. I broke a lot of Edward's favorite things. I smashed in the computer screen with a heavy trophy."

"Cool. Good for you. May I ask with whom he's having the affair?" Carrie couldn't help being nosy.

"Had. He had an affair. Past tense. It's over. That's what he's promised."

"I can't believe he started one in the first place. He always seems so devoted to you."

Annie was irate now. "He didn't start it. She did. She's a hussy who goes after other women's husbands. She's done this before in Sun View."

"Who is it? Anyone I know?" Carrie could not contain her curiosity.

"You won't believe who it is. It's Beverly Sangelo. She's the one who's running for a spot on the board."

"On our Community Association Board of Directors?"

"Yes, she was running. She won't be when I get done with her," Annie said while shaking her fist.

"What are you going to do?" Carrie asked.

"I'm going to tell what she's done to as many people as I can. I'm going to write a letter to the editor of the Sun. I'm going to show up at the Meet the Candidates night and tell the crowd the whole story. I'm smearing her reputation." Annie had gone again from being sad to being very angry.

"Aren't you afraid this will reflect badly on you?"

"I don't give a damn. I hate that bitch. She's ruined my life. I don't deserve this in my so-called Golden Years. Evidently, when I was gone to Sarasota, she dragged him all over town—on her walk each morning and to her dance class, for example. I am so humiliated. I can't face any of my friends."

***

Carrie called Judy and told her about Annie's woes right after Annie left. A week later Judy dropped in for her usual weekly visit, poured herself a cup of coffee, and helped herself to the last of the coffee cake sitting on the table. "I meant to call you about yesterday's conversation with Annie, but I forgot. What's the latest?"

"Well, the latest is that the President of the Community Association has told Annie that he will not get involved. He feels it's a private matter. She wanted him to tell Beverly that she can't run for a seat on the board. Now Annie's trying to get a lot of her friends to put pressure on him. I personally don't want to take a stand." Carrie felt bad about not helping her friend, but she just didn't want to get involved.

Judy said, "I don't understand why she's so angry at Beverly. It takes two to tango, you know. I'd be using a 2 x 4 on my husband."

"I know I wondered about that. You know Edward was a traveling salesman. I'm sure he had lots of temptations along the way. If he strayed, he must have been good at keeping it from Annie. She's just sure he is a poor, defenseless guy who got seduced by a very bad woman."

"I guess she needs to think that in order to go on living with him and getting through this," Judy said. "I say, when a woman steals your husband, there is no better revenge than to let her keep him."

Carrie started recalling her past. "You know, I was the other woman several times in my life. Believe me, I never had to seduce anyone. The men were out there looking when they found me. I read the book Married Men Make the Best Lovers by Ruth Dickson."

"Whoa. I thought you said you didn't seduce anyone. That sounds like you were studying how to get a married man," Judy said, wondering what her friend had been up to.

"No, I read it as a lark, but it had a whole lot of truths in it."

"Like what?" Judy knew they were off the subject of Annie, but she wanted to know why a married man, who is not free, makes a better lover."

Carrie tried to explain. "The book has very little to do with the physical side of a relationship. It's about all the other aspects. It's about being adored. Married men are very appreciative. And very generous, which I think comes from feeling guilty about using up the other woman without being able to give her a legitimate and permanent place in his life. The other woman gets to see him when he's at his best."

"It sounds like an interesting book," Judy said, with a smile. "Do you still have it?"

"Yes, I suppose it's around here somewhere, but don't get any ideas, Judy."

"Okay. Tell me the rest of the story of Annie."

Carrie shook her head. "That's pretty much it. Annie did say that Edward and Beverly only made love once."

"Yeah, right." Judy was definitely not buying that one.

***

Annie was much calmer now, several weeks later. "Can you believe she got elected? If they hadn't cut me off at the Meet the Candidates night before I was able to tell the whole story, she would have been run out of town. She is so phony but has a lot of people fooled. Anyway, I don't care. She doesn't have my husband any more."

Carrie asked, "How can you be sure?"

"Because I don't let him out of my sight. I go everywhere with him. Before I was giving him way too much freedom. In fact, I would leave him for a week or two to go visit my daughter in Sarasota. Now he goes with me or I don't go."

"Do you two like living that way with so much togetherness?"

"Look, I'm not losing my husband. I'm not dividing our property, and I'm not giving up my home. Whatever it takes. Edward is so apologetic he'll do anything I say. See this beautiful bracelet he bought me? I feel he's really sorry. He tells me he's so embarrassed he got involved with Beverly."

"I'm glad there's a happy ending to this," Carrie said.

"Not without a lot of work and heartache. We've been seeing a counselor, and that's helping. The children are starting to speak to Edward again. They were so mad at him. I'm okay some days. Other days I'm very depressed. It's hard to forgive and forget."

"You probably won't ever forget, but think of it as a sore. At first it's a painful, open wound. After time passes, the wound heals and the pain is gone, but there'll always be a scar." Carrie hoped these words would touch Annie's heart. She truly hoped for the best for her friend.

When Judy left, Carrie headed for the refrigerator to make herself a hot fudge sundae. As she sat at the table, savoring every bite of the cold ice cream, she got a lump in her throat and realized she was depressed. She wondered how many wives she had taken to the brink of despair by being the other woman. *I rationalized it by saying that the men were looking when they found me, but if all the "other" women of the world had turned them down, they wouldn't have had the opportunity to be unfaithful. However, if I go down this path of thinking, I'll need a shrink. Snap out it.*

Carrie vowed then and there that, no matter how lonely she was, she wouldn't take up with a married man again. And she would do everything possible to ascertain his true marital status before going out with him, even on the first date. Those thoughts and resolutions made her feel better, and she put down the spoon to the sundae. She decided that she didn't need to medicate her depression with food.

'Til I Can't Take It Anymore

"Hi there, gorgeous!"

Carrie knew this conversation was going to go well with such a nice start. She turned around and saw a tall, dark, handsome stranger standing there with a huge smile. Maybe this singles dance isn't going to be so bad after all. Marilyn, a gal she had met recently, had talked her into going along as Carrie had mentioned she was tired of watching HGTV and the Comedy Channel and was looking for something to do.

"Hello. You certainly know how to make an old woman feel good although I don't believe you for a second." Carrie wished she hadn't used the phrase "old woman." No need to remind anyone. She was finally to the age where she cared about her age. She certainly wasn't old enough to be bragging about her age as she heard some women around town do. She reminded herself never to use the word "old" or tell her age to anyone any more.

"I do need to come up with another opening line, don't I? I mean, you are very pretty and all but I don't want to be corny."

"It's okay. I'm glad to make your acquaintance. I'm Caroline Bolton, but everyone calls me Carrie."

"I'm Alex Krug, newly arrived to town. And you do remind me of Rhonda Fleming."

Rhonda Fleming! Crap. She's a hundred years old or been dead for 40 years. He could have at least said a young Rhonda Fleming.

"Well, I hope you love Sun View as much as I do."

Alex said, "I've actually been here a year, but this is the first singles dance I've come to. Do you go to many?"

"No, I rarely go. I don't know why. I just have a lot of other things to do.

I volunteer a lot. *I don't want to tell him I try other ways to get laid.* Where do you live?"

"I have a house on Wolf Laurel that I share with another guy."

Just as the words "GAY, GAY-ER, GAY-EST" were throbbing through Carrie's brain, Marilyn came up and announced that she and Carrie had to go home as she was not feeling well.

Alex said that he hoped that they would meet again. He actually said that he thought Carrie was just swell, that he was delighted to make her acquaintance, and kissed her hand with grand flourish.

***

Carrie telephoned her friend Judy first thing the next morning. "Remind me to never go to a singles dance again."

"What happened?"

"I met a guy named Alex. He seemed sort of nice, although a little flamboyant."

"He could have worse things wrong with him," Judy said.

"Like most men I meet, he has a gigantic flaw and of course, I'm attracted to him. He lives with another man here in town."

"Oh, oh. Gay. That is a problem," Judy said.

"No, I don't think he's gay. Why would he be at a singles dance? As far as I know, that's not where gay men meet other gay men."

"Could he be a switch-hitter?"

"Maybe. But that's not his flaw."

"Well, what is it?" Judy was very curious now.

"I'm not going to say yet. I'm going to see if it bothers me."

***

Alex managed to remember Carrie's first and last name and looked her up in the town's membership directory. He called her, and they had several dates. Alex turned out to be a very interesting and kind man. He continued to be flamboyant, but she ignored that aspect of his personality. It actually seemed kind of charming to her.

She had also learned to overlook his coal-black hair. It couldn't possibly be natural, but it didn't look dyed. In fact, it looked good with his unlined, youthful skin. Still there's THE flaw. His flaw continued to bother her, but she kept trying to get past it.

"How did you come to move to Sun View and buy a house with another man?" Carrie decided to be bold and just ask one of many questions on her mind.

"My roommate was dumped by his wife recently. I have never been married. We both wanted to come to a retirement community. It just made sense to move in together. I'm sure everyone thinks we're gay, but we're not."

Okay, we've crossed one big hurdle. I wish his big flaw would be this easily dismissed. "Why didn't a good-looking guy like you get married?"

"I spent several years in my family's uniform business. Then I had to suddenly take it over when my father became ill. I was always busy. I dated some but just never met the right gal. My family is one big, happy Catholic family. No lady ever seemed to fit in.

The dates that Alex and Carrie had were always ended with a goodnight kiss, nothing more. Alex seemed to be the perfect gentleman. A little too perfect, Carrie thought. Maybe that's why he never got to marriage; he never passed first base.

Carrie was surprised when Alex invited her to a Super Bowl party that he and his roommate were having in their home. She didn't understand how he could know so many people so soon. Obviously, not too many people were turned off by his BIG FLAW.

"Well, there're two of us, and we both have outgoing personalities. We've just met lots of people in a year. Besides, it's not going to be that big of a party. We're just going to eat, drink, and watch the game."

At the party, Carrie made conversation with the folks there. She was dreading the start of the game as she doesn't like football. She can never figure out who has the ball. She liked the pre-game commentary, the opening ceremonies, and all the cute commercials so she figured she could get through the evening without looking bored. At half-time, Alex whispered to her, "You're not really into this game, are you, Carrie?"

"Oh, I'm sorry. Is it that obvious? I just don't understand the game, but I like being with you and everyone."

Alex winked at Carrie as he often did, and said, "Wait here a minute while I get something out of my bedroom." As he passed his roommate, he whispered something to him. His roommate just nodded.

When Alex reentered the room, he announced to the crowd that he and Carrie were going to take a walk. They walked for about a block and then turned around.

"Where are we going?" Carrie couldn't figure out why they were heading back.

It was dark now and no one could see them walk around to the back of Alex's home. He opened his bedroom window, the one he had evidently unlocked earlier, urged her to be quiet, and helped her climb through the window. Carrie finally caught on that Alex was trying to protect her honor by being so surreptitious.

Without turning on the lights, Alex swept Carrie into his arms. His passion that had lain dormant for several weeks was in full operation now. He quickly undressed her and himself, and they made love on his bed. He was a very considerate, skillful lover. *Thank God, he's not so Catholic he won't wear a condom. I still haven't got this gay idea out of my mind although he doesn't seem too gay tonight.*

***

"Damn, damn, damn," Carrie said to Judy. "This is my usual luck."

"What's wrong?"

"I just can't get past it. He has it all. He's nice, interesting, charming, good-looking, considerate. He's got frigging everything."

"But the one big flaw?" Judy asked.

"Right. The one big flaw."

"Well, are you going to tell me what it is yet?"

"Okay, here it goes. Why did God do this to him? Why didn't he get it fixed. You see, Judy, he's cross-eyed!"

"What? You mean he has a wayward eye, don't you?"

"No, Judy, he's just plain old cross-eyed. One eye is more crossed than the other one, I think. I've never analyzed it too much, because I have a hard time looking at him. I'm just going to stop dating him. I feel everyone is making fun of him until they get to know him. I don't think I can go through the rest of life thinking that."

"So adios?" Judy asked.

"Adios, dear, sweet, cross-eyed Alex."

Dust on the Bible

Carrie hurried over to the Fitness Center. She wanted some time in the walking pool before her first meeting. The walking pool was a wonderful idea for retirees. Carrie wasn't as old as most of the walkers, but it suited her as she didn't like to get her shoulder-length hair wet. The pool was exercise but not strenuous, which also suited her. The water was the same depth—3 ½ to 4 ½ feet—in the entire pool. Men and women would get in the pool and all walk in the same direction, round and round. Sometimes this seemed almost ludicrous, but it was fun, especially as the walkers talked a lot. There would be clusters of two or three, chattering away as they moved around the pool.

As she arrived, she wondered what was going on outside of the Fitness Center. There were about ten people waiting to buy tickets. She joined the end of the line to find out what was happening.

She tapped the tall man in front of her on the arm. "What's going on?"

As he turned around, their eyes met and there were instant fireworks. "Whoa, beautiful, where'd you come from?"

"I wanted to find out what's happening." Carrie couldn't take her eyes off of this guy. He was a big one, very tall and beefy. He had a handsome face, full of sunshine. Her heart was racing. In the ensuing conversation she realized that he was a happy, somewhat-boisterous type. He was quick to introduce himself.

"I'm Jerry, but feel free to call me Jerry."

Okay, he's corny but nice, Carrie thought.

"This is the line to buy tickets to the fundraiser for the Hamiltons," Jerry explained. "They're down on their luck, and a lot of people are trying to help them."

Carrie and Jerry continued to talk as they moved up the line. Finally, reaching the table, Carrie, wanting to help too, bought herself a single ticket. They were ten dollars, but she figured she could afford it for a good cause. Besides, she would look foolish if she talked with Jerry for five minutes in line and then didn't buy a ticket.

"Where are you headed now? To work out?" Jerry didn't seem too anxious to end their encounter.

"The walking pool. You ought to try it some time. It's fun to walk and talk."

As they parted, Jerry said, "Maybe I will."

***

Carrie tried to use the walking pool five times a week. Any morning she didn't have an early appointment, she was there at nine o'clock when it opened. As she circled around in the pool, she was lost in thoughts of Jerry. He's such a neat guy. Too bad he has a little circle of gold on the ring finger of his left hand. Married! Just my luck.

"Hello, beautiful. I can't believe I can't remember your name."

Oh no, it's Jerry. How'd he get into the pool without my seeing him? Not only is he married, he's senile. Can't remember my name.

"Gee, I must have really impressed you. You can't remember my name." Carrie said. "Remember, my name's Carrie."

"Carrie, I was so taken with you that I probably wouldn't have known my own name when we were in line."

"You knew it. You told me it was Jerry."

"Gosh, I'm glad I got it right." Jerry laughed much louder than his little joke deserved.

Jerry and Carrie walked and talked. In fact, they walked and talked every day for three weeks. She found out that he had been a traveling salesman and then a sales manager in Virginia, his home state before retiring. Jerry was quick to explain that he was not the usual kind of traveling salesman, not the kind described in many jokes.

"I'm a God-fearin', Christian man. I go to church every Sunday, and I try to live a good life. I traveled the highways and back roads of Virginia, West

Virginia, and Tennessee and never once cut out on my wife."

Carrie found out that he was a talented singer. "Do you sing Country?"

"I sure do. You like Country, huh? Maybe I'll sing for you. I mostly perform gospel in churches around here, but if you want country, I'll croon a country tune for you." With that, Jerry burst into song. And, of course, it would have to be her all time favorite song, "Crazy". He didn't sound like Willie Nelson, who wrote the song, nor did he sound like Patsy Cline, who made it a classic, but he sounded very good. All the little clusters of people stopped their talking and listened to him while they continued walking in the pool. At the end they all applauded. He was good.

"Now, if you say you can yodel, I'll know you're the perfect man for me," Carrie said, laughing and realizing she shouldn't have said that.

"Guess what? I can yodel." To prove his point, he began singing "I Want to Be a Cowboy's Sweetheart." Not exactly an appropriate song for a man to sing, but that was the only song with yodeling he could think of at the moment. Once again, he turned in a flawless performance. Now everyone in the pool was buzzing. Who is this guy and why is he singing? Jerry and Carrie were oblivious of them, though, being caught up in their own tête-à-tête.

"I could listen to you for a very long time," Carrie said.

"I'd like to sing for you for a very long time. Why don't we get out of the pool and go have a late breakfast?" Jerry sounded so very happy Carrie didn't want to disappoint him so she agreed. He was exactly the take-charge type she liked, the kind who would make decisions for her so she could rest after years of making all of her own decisions.

Carrie laughed to herself when Jerry picked the Burger King drive-thru for their late breakfast. He chose sausage, egg, and cheese Croisanwiches, orange juice, coffee, and cinnamon rolls to top it off. Then he pulled into the parking lot behind the Burger King where there were several trees to shade the car. They rolled down the windows and began devouring their food.

After eating, Jerry began singing again. Carrie loved the music and the attention. He was singing just for her. After a while, Jerry said, "I'm so lucky. God chose me to have a wonderful voice and impart joy in other people's lives. Music can be powerful. The minister always has me sing right before he asks for those who want to be saved, or to join the church, to come forward. Many go forward with tears in their eyes from my song. I feel I'm ministering too."

All of a sudden, Carrie realized what was happening. She thought he wanted to save her. She was sure Jerry brought her here to talk religion. Jerry took her hand. *This is it. What will I do? I don't want to be saved. I have my own religion. I just want out of here.*

With his other hand, he pulled her close to him. *This is an interesting way to be saved.* He let go of her hand and lifted her face to his. *Maybe I'm going to be baptized with spit. Oh no, I'm going to be kissed. What's going on?* Jerry kissed Carrie tenderly at first and then fervently.

"Carrie, I know this is wrong, but I just can't help myself. I'm so attracted to you. I'm still just a Virginia hick. Oh, I learned a few manners along the way and learned to dress the part of a sales manager, but I'm really just a poor country boy. You're so sophisticated, something I've wanted to be all my life. I love your polish. I want to better myself, and I want you by my side. Anyway, I think of you night and day. I can't wait to get to the pool each day. If you're not there, my day is ruined. Oh, God, please help me. Now I guess I understand the ministers who fall by the wayside."

"No, this won't work. Does your wife know about me?" Carrie said this to snap Jerry back to reality.

"Billie Jean knows I go to the pool and talk with others. She doesn't know the "others" is you. She is a wonderful lady, and I don't want to hurt her."

"Jerry, I find you extremely attractive. I'm very fond of you. I think of you a lot, a lot more than I should. This is very painful for me to say, but I don't want to start anything. I have not lived a wonderfully pure life, but I couldn't live with myself if I were the one to bring down a nice, lovely, Christian man like you. And you are a very nice man. I admire you and what you stand for. There should be a lot more men like you. This world would be a lot better off."

At this point, Jerry began to cry, softly at first then in large sobbing gasps. "Oh, God, please forgive me. Oh, please, dear God. Carrie, please forgive me. What have I done?"

"You know God will forgive you, Jerry. No damage has been done. Take me back to my car now, and we'll part as friends. Okay?"

***

It took all the willpower Carrie had, but she managed to stay away from the walking pool for a month. She wondered if Jerry went there. Her curiosity almost got the best of her several times. She felt cruel, breaking up the relationship this way, but it had to be done. For his sake and for hers.

In a couple of months Carrie ran into Jerry and Billie Jean at, of all places, the entrance to the Fitness Center where they had met. Jerry introduced the two women, and they carried on a conversation for a few minutes. He explained to his wife that Carrie was a woman he had met and talked with in the walking pool. As they were getting ready to go, Jerry gave Carrie a big bear hug and whispered in her ear, "Thank you and God bless you for what you did."

For once Carrie felt like she had done the right thing. It still hurt, though. And she was still incredibly lonely. She wiped a tear from her eye and headed toward the walking pool.

I Want to be Wanted

"Well, I'm finally excited about something, Judy."

"What's that?" Judy assumed that Carrie had met a new man. "Mr. Wonderful has finally entered your life, right?"

Carrie was red in the face and practically hyperventilating. "No, sireee, I won a contest. I won a four-day cruise out of Tampa. Can you believe it?"

Judy was wary. "Are you sure it's not some sort of come-on?"

"No, Judy. I really did win. I won! I won! You know I enter a lot of contests online every day. It's my first-thing-in-the-morning ritual. Well, I finally won one of them. I've won lots of little things but never anything this big."

"That's nice. Congratulations. When do you leave?"

"We leave whenever we want," Carrie explained.

"We? Whom are you taking? Is the trip for two?"

"Yeah, the contest trips are always for two, and guess what? I'm taking you."

"Me? Me? Why aren't you taking some man?" Judy thought that was an obvious question. Carrie always liked to have a man by her side.

"If you haven't noticed, there's not exactly anyone sailing on my loveboat right now. Get excited, Judy. You're going."

***

"I'm sure glad that's over. It's scary hearing what we have to do in case of a disaster on board the ship." This was Judy's first cruise and she wasn't wild about the safety drill the cruise line has everyone go through right at the beginning of the trip.

"It's over and there won't be any more Titanic talk for four days. Relax and enjoy yourself." Carrie was acting like the big sister to Judy as she had been on several cruises and knew the routine. "Did you see that guy watching us during the drill?"

"Omigod, Carrie, you haven't found a man already, have you? He probably just wondered why we were attending the drill as we both look buoyant enough to float without a life jacket."

Carrie laughed. "Wait 'til you see all the food there is to eat. You haven't seen buoyant yet. Wait 'til you see how much you gain on this trip. Let's go get something to drink."

"Where do we go?" Judy asked.

"There are lots of bars on board, but let's pick one where we can watch the ship set sail."

***

The ship was underway. The sun rays twinkled on the beautiful blue water. Carrie, and especially Judy, were mesmerized by the sight and just sat and watched for the longest time. Finally, they both ordered the drink of the day—a Virgin's Downfall.

"I got this drink for you, Judy. You're practically a virgin again, aren't you? What with very few, if any, dates lately." Judy didn't appreciate Carrie's attempt at humor.

Their reverie was broken when a tall, distinguished-looking gentleman came to their table and said, "Your husbands shouldn't leave two beautiful women all alone in a bar."

"And why would that be?" Carrie had quickly hushed Judy before she blurted out that they weren't married. Carrie had recognized the guy as the one who was watching them at the drill earlier.

"Two unescorted ladies will be hit on by lonely men like me," he said, with eyes twinkling. "My name's Cedric. May I join you?"

Cedric! What the hell kind of name is that? Carrie thought. This guy is phony baloney. All he needs is an ascot. "Sure, sit down. You're a good-looking guy. I doubt that you'll be lonely for long, Cedric."

"Where are you two from?" Cedric asked. "By the way, you can call me

Rick. That's my nickname. My mother had an affair with a movie star named Cedric and was always in love with him, so the story goes. That's how I got my name."

"Rick, we're from Florida."

"So am I. Where in Florida?"

"A little town called Sun View."

"You won't believe this! I live in Sun View too. There are a lot of Sun View residents on this trip. Some sort of tour or something," Rick explained. "Are you part of the tour?"

"No, we're not." Carrie wasn't ready to tell Rick too much about herself, including how she got on this cruise.

"Do you ladies own homes in Sun View?"

"Yes, we do." Judy said, before she picked up on Carrie's closed-mouth technique.

Sensing Carrie and Judy's wariness, Rick said, "Well, I've got to go to a different lounge now. I'll see you gals later. You two are single, aren't you?"

"Maybe," was all Carrie said.

After Rick left, Judy said, "Why were you so guarded with him, Carrie? I mean he lives in Sun View. How dangerous can he be?"

"Judy, there are child molesters living in Sun View."

"Carrie, don't worry. You no longer qualify as a child."

"You know what I mean. You never know what kind of a pervert lives around the corner from you. Even in Sun View."

***

Dinner was nice. There were two couples and two single gals along with Carrie and Judy at the dinner table. The conversation was interesting, finding out where everyone was from and how this cruise was comparing to others the group had been on. After dinner, Carrie and Judy headed for another lounge that was supposed to be playing big band music. Carrie liked Country music, but Judy was lost in the 40s although that decade was way before her time. Judy dreamed of living in a simpler time and loved the 30s and 40s, especially the music.

They slid around the big purple tufted seat that was in a semi-circle around a black lacquer round table. Everything on this ship was posh. This lounge was no exception. The room was dark except for the spotlights aimed at the dance floor. Couples waltzed around to the music. Occasionally, there would be a jitterbug number.

"Oh, no, there's Rick. How did we get so lucky to pick the one lounge he would be in?" Carrie asked. Her sarcasm wasn't lost on Judy.

"I don't know, but I will say he's a really smooth dancer. Look at him dip that woman at the end of the dance."

Finally, Carrie had to admit to herself that Rick was a good dancer, really good. She had watched him dance about five numbers in a row, each with a different partner. She was hoping he wouldn't see Judy and herself sitting there. Carrie didn't consider herself a very good dancer, and she sure didn't want to dance with Mr. Fred Astaire.

"Ladies, we meet again. Would one of you care to dance?"

"Not me," Judy piped up. "I don't dance."

"I don't want to dance either. I'm not very good," Carrie said.

"Come on, Carrie. I will make you look good. Just relax and follow my lead," Rick said.

Sure enough, Rick could make Carrie look good. He was a very strong leader, and Carrie actually found herself enjoying dancing around the room. She enjoyed being the center of attention, as they were the best dancers on the floor.

"How did you get so good at dancing?" Carrie asked.

"This is my profession," Rick replied.

"Your profession? You're a professional dancer?

"No, I just get a lot of practice. The cruise line pays me to dance with all the unescorted ladies."

Carrie thought about this for a while. "Oh," she finally said, "don't you need to dance with some of the other ladies?"

"No, Carrie, I can dance with whomever I please. I find you a lovely, charming woman. You're definitely way above the others."

"Charming? How can you say that? I've been very guarded in my conversation with you all day. I've not been myself."

"I know you're just protecting yourself. It doesn't pay for an attractive, wealthy lady to take up with just anyone on shipboard," Rick explained.

"Wealthy? How do you know I'm wealthy?" Carrie asked.

"I can smell wealth. I've had a lot of experience.

The two of them danced many dances, only taking out time for a couple of drinks the whole evening. Judy had headed back to her cabin long ago. Carrie felt bad about leaving her friend alone but was having too much fun to quit. Judy would understand. She always did. Carrie was giddy from the drinks, the dances, and all the attention Rick was paying her. She decided that he wasn't so bad after all. He had possibilities.

"I can't go to your room and you can't come to mine. That's against company policy. However, I know a little out-of-the-way lounge that's very dark. We can have our privacy for a little conversation. How about it?"

***

The next two days were spent much the same as the first day. Rick had managed to get himself transferred to their dinner table. One of the husbands at the table had gotten seasick and was spending all of his time in his cabin, taking no meals in the dining room so there was a space at the table. Rick was a charming dinner companion with lots of stories so no one minded.

Rick, Carrie, and Judy were together all through the days. Rick continued to ask lots of questions of both women. Carrie and Judy continued to be very vague. Judy managed to get lost at night so that Rick and Carrie could dance a lot and be alone. Occasionally, Rick would dance with other women just to look like he was doing his job, but his eyes were always on Carrie. They ended each evening in the dark little bar Rick liked for privacy, as he called it. By now, Carrie was definitely falling for Rick.

***

One of ladies who sat at Carrie and Judy's dinner table stopped by their breakfast table on the last morning of the cruise. "May I join you for a moment?"

"Sure, have a seat. We're just ordering now."

"I can't stay. I just wanted to talk with you for a minute. It's none of my business but you're such nice ladies that I think you should know."

"Know what?" Carrie asked.

"I've noticed that you and Rick have hit it off quite well. So, to be blunt, let me tell you that Rick is a gigolo."

"What?" Both Judy and Carrie said in unison.

"Yes, he lives off of wealthy women. I guess he makes love to them too. What I do know is he definitely spends their money. A lot of people know this. We've seen him in operation on other cruises. Just be careful."

Carrie didn't know whether to laugh or cry. Then she started laughing, softly at first, then louder. "I know I look like an idiot, Judy, but the last laugh is on Rick. I don't have a cent of extra money. I can barely support myself. The only way I can go on a cruise is to win it. So long, Rick, my great shipboard romance."

I Was Born the Running Kind

"I think I've met the man of my dreams," Judy said as she pushed her way through the door of Carrie's kitchen.

"What! That's great, Judy. Give me the scoop!"

"Well, you know how I go to the singles dances here in town occasionally?"

"Yes, it seems to be your only social life, but I hope that doesn't sound cruel," Carrie said, wishing she hadn't been so honest.

"Never mind. You can't burst my bubble today. This guy asked me to dance. And then he asked me to dance again. Finally, we ended up dancing to every number. When the band went home, we continued talking over coffee for hours. We seem to have a lot in common."

"Like what?"

"Both of us have lost our spouses of many years, and both have three children whom we're supporting."

"Oh, a match made in heaven," Carrie said sarcastically. "Why would you even bring up the fact you're supporting three grown children? Oh well, it seems to have worked out. What's his name?"

"Alan Johnson"

Carrie almost passed out. "Alan Johnson?"

"Yeah. Why do you know him?" Judy asked.

"No, no, I don't know him." Carrie found herself telling a big, fat, white lie. She had dated Alan about six or seven times. She would never, ever tell Judy this. She promised herself she would go to the grave with this secret. He was a nice enough guy, but there were several things about him she didn't like. She wondered how Judy was going to handle one of his idiosyncrasies. The guy liked long sexual sessions with lots of strange positions. He wore

Carrie out. She often wished that there had been a trapeze over the bed or all sorts of bars on the bed so she could hold on while he screwed her upside down, downside up, inside out, and every other way he could imagine.

I'm glad someone's love life is going well." Carrie wanted to take the conversation away from Alan Johnson as fast as she could. She was afraid she would slip up and give her secret away.

"What's wrong now, Carrie?" Judy dropped her excitement of finding a man to listen to Carrie's woes.

"Frankly, I'm lonely. There must be someone out there for me. I shouldn't be sitting home every night listening to the same Eddie Arnold CD while reading email. He was a great country singer, you know, and I love the old-time artists like him. Also, I'm excited I've found a station of Classic Country on the Internet, but I sit in at my desk and outside there's a life that moves without me."

"Okay, okay. Back to the subject at hand...maybe God thinks you've been through your share of men and is leaving the rest to us less fortunate women."

"You're probably right. I think I'll switch to women. There's evidently a large supply of them available everywhere."

"You wouldn't dare. Really? Would you?"

Seeing the seriousness of Carrie's expression, Judy wasn't sure she was kidding.

"It's not a dare because I've always been a closet bisexual."

"What? You've got to be kidding," Judy answered, shocked.

"You know what Rodney Dangerfield said about bisexuality—it immediately doubles your chances for a date on Saturday night. Just kidding. Don't get worried, Judy. You've always been a good friend but not my type."

"That's a big relief! Then why do you always date men?"

"Because I prefer men to women; I like their equipment better. But. that doesn't mean I couldn't have a successful relationship with a woman."

"Including sex?"

"Including sex. Have you forgotten my short-lived Lesbian relationship in the Navy."

"I guess I did, but I just thought it was experimentation and you had learned your lesson." Judy had almost forgotten the story Carrie had revealed to her about her secret trysts with a female candidate in the Navy. Finally, she remembered Carrie's story about officer candidate school in Rhode Island."

Judy continued, "Never mind. I'm more interested in getting some useful advice about keeping this man I've just rounded up. You must do something right to attract so many men...and do I have to add 'women' now?"

"You're asking for advice from me? Exactly how drunk are you?" Carrie kiddingly asked. Judy had poured herself a drink, but Carrie knew she wasn't drunk.

"You don't want advice from a friend with a track record like mine."

"Yes, I do. You know you're much more sophisticated in the world of men than I am."

"Okay, but I can't guarantee results. Now you consider me to be a fairly liberated gal, right?"

"Right," Judy answered.

"I've had a career in a man's field, supporting myself successfully for many years. I've been single for much of my life, taking care of all financial and domestic things for myself. Right?"

"I agree. What's this got to do with anything?" Judy didn't understand.

"Well, what I'm going to tell you would frost the nuts of most women's libbers." Carrie was getting wound up now and mixing metaphors.

"Interesting expression. Go ahead."

"You have to take care of a man from the kitchen to the bedroom. Just being a good cook isn't enough of a good thing. Giving blowjobs is even more important. A lot of older women won't do it, but there isn't a man around that doesn't love it."

"Yuck."

"See what I mean. You need to get past that and just do it. I love to give them. I don't know why, but they really turn me on." She knew Judy was going to need this particular skill with Alan.

"Okay, okay, forget the details; there's surely more to it than cooking and blowing," Judy said with "yuck" still stuck in her throat. "There's a lot of time between meals and sex. Besides I'm more interested in getting him to a meal before I can jump in bed. First things first."

"That part's easy. Most men, like most people—men and women—are more interested in themselves than anyone else. Some are self-absorbed because they lack confidence and are constantly wondering if they're doing everything right. Some are just self-centered. Anyway, what you have to do is feed that ego first."

"Oh, Lordy. I've never learned the ooh and ahh routine."

"You don't have to. In fact, you don't necessarily have to be dishonest. All you do is keep the conversation focused on your man. You ask questions about him or about what he's saying." Carrie couldn't believe that most women didn't understand this. "Actually, it's the fine art of conversation with most of the attention turned on the man. If he asks a question about you, answer it, but then turn the conversation back to him."

"And that works?" Judy thought she understood.

"This new love of yours will think you are the greatest conversationalist around and think you really understand him. At least he'll know that you are really interested in him without your ever having said so."

Judy asked, "So why hasn't this worked for you? You still don't have a man."

"Correction. I don't have a man to keep. I never have trouble in getting them or having them hang around for a while. Most are just not lasting relationships."

"Maybe you should do more than conversing, cooking, and blowing."

"No, that's not my problem. My problem is that I always fall for the 'bad boy' types. They seem to attract me. 'Good boys' bore me. But then I find out the bad boys are a little too bad. They have some serious kind of character flaw, just as I've explained in the many stories I've told you. I have to bail out before they take me down with them."

"Interesting," said Judy.

"Don't ask me for advice. I'm all messed up, so I don't think I qualify to help you. Just go and enjoy your new romance and tell him that Carrie sent you."

The two girls laughed and hugged. Carrie was really overjoyed that some happiness had come into Judy's life.

After Judy left, Carrie sat, wondering if things would had turned out differently if she hadn't been so anxious to jump in bed with the guys she dated. She screwed a lot of men on the first date. What would have happened if she had been coy and insisted on waiting until there was a strong emotional attachment? Then she got to wondering why she felt like she wanted to get in bed so quickly. Did she get turned on faster than most women? Or was she wanting to feel like she belonged to someone? Mistaking sex for affection and acceptance? A therapist once told her belonging was the opposite of loneliness. There's that loneliness thing again. Always rearing its ugly head, Carrie thought.

I Don't Really Want to Know

It was Christmastime, and Carrie was happy. This was one of her favorite times of the year, even in Florida. She was lonely and wished that she had someone with whom to share her happiness and the holidays, but she had decided to stop her big hunt for Mr. Wonderful. Too many maladjusted men out there, she thought.

As she pulled into the Winn-Dixie parking lot, she was glad that she'd decided to invite some single friends over for a Christmas meal. It was fun planning, shopping for, and preparing a big meal again. She told all of the invited guests that they shouldn't bring any food. She wanted to do the whole meal for 14 people herself. There was something therapeutic in cooking a meal that she knew would be a big hit with her friends. Carrie had decided to look for ways in which she could have a rich life without a special man at her side.

"Please donate to the Salvation Army," a tall Santa Claus said as he rang a bell.

"Sure," Carrie said as she dug in her handbag for her coin purse. Donating to the Salvation Army was a usual part of her Christmas routine, and she was glad to contribute again this year.

"Come on, you can give more than a dollar," Santa said, startling Carrie.

The surprised look on her face prompted Santa to add, "Any lady who has as much gold jewelry on as you, can certainly afford to give more than a dollar."

"Well, okay, but I can honestly say that I've never been intimidated by a Salvation Army Santa before." She slipped a five dollar bill into the kettle and entered the store, wondering if the Salvation Army knew that this volunteer Santa was badgering people.

***

Carrie's Christmas meal was a big success as she knew it would be. It was fun to be with all of her friends. There was a lot of gaiety even though each person was without his or her family this holiday time. After a leisurely meal followed by coffee and dessert, everyone gathered around Carrie's piano and sang carols. Then everyone left, agreeing that this should be an annual event. Everyone left, that is, except Peter who timed a trip to the bathroom so that he would still be there after everyone else departed.

"I wanted to stay so I could ask a favor of you in private," Peter said.

"What is it?" Peter was a very close friend of Carrie's. They tried dating once, but it didn't work out right from the start because Carrie quickly realized that Peter had a commitment phobia. He just wanted to play around, be a Condo Cowboy, as he put it. This wasn't for Carrie, and she bailed out after just a couple of dates. But because Peter was such a nice and fun guy, he and Carrie had developed a very wonderful friendship. Carrie enjoyed listening to Peter tell of his adventures and misadventures trying to juggle four or five women at the same time.

"Will you go with me to the Samaritan Ball?"

"What? Why would you want me to go with you when you have all these women who, if they knew, would be dying to go?" Carrie was truly puzzled.

"Well, as you know, the ball is a very expensive affair. I don't want to give any one of the ladies the wrong idea by spending that much money on her. Besides, they give a lot of publicity to the affair afterwards, and I don't want to show up in the paper with a date. Everyone knows that you and I are just very good friends."

"Why even go in the first place?"

"It's payback to the organizer of the ball. I owe her a big favor, and she has called it in, getting me to buy tickets."

"Okay, I'll go."

***

The Samaritan Ball was the elegant affair that it always was. The event made a lot of money even though the designers spent a lot of money decorating the ballroom to the hilt. The guys all wore tuxedos, and the gals all saved their best gowns or bought new ones for this event. Carrie was in a beautiful aqua gown that she knew enhanced her red hair and skin coloring. She was lucky that her hair had not yet turned gray even though she had just turned fifty-eight.

"Hello, lovely lady. Still handing out dollar bills?"

"Excuse me? Do I know you?"

"It's Santa. You know, the one that razzed you about donating a dollar when it appeared that you could certainly afford more."

"I see you don't give all of your money to charity either. That's no ordinary tux you rented. It looks like it's custom-made out of fine fabric." Carrie tried razzing him back.

"I didn't rent this; it's mine. I'm on the board of Samaritan Services so I thought I should show up and look presentable."

"Well, have a nice evening," Carrie said as she returned to her table. She thought Santa was impertinent.

Peter and Carrie danced a few dances but mostly just talked with the others at their table. Later, as Santa walked by, Peter said, "See that guy there? He struck up a conversation with me at the bar. Talk quickly turned to you. I could tell he was trying to find out what relationship you and I have."

"I hope you didn't tell him."

"Yes, I did."

"Oh, Lordy. He's a drip."

"Well, here comes the drip, headed for our table."

"May I have this dance, lovely lady?" This guy was good looking, but so far he seemed like a pain in the butt. Carrie couldn't think of an excuse fast enough. Before she knew it, she was in his arms, swirling around the floor in a waltz.

"You can stop calling me 'Lovely Lady.' My name's Carrie."

"Mine is Thomas Drake Worthington IV."

"I didn't ask, but I have heard of your family. They've donated a lot to the arts in Tampa, right?"

Ignoring her question, he said, "You don't like me much, do you?"

"Well, so far, I haven't been too impressed."

"I'm just a nice guy, trying to get by in this world."

"Right, Thomas Drake Worthngton IV. I bet you've never had a job in your life. You just live off of granddaddy's money. Or was it great granddaddy's?"

"It was Great Grandpa Worthington's ambition and luck that paid off big time. However, I do work very hard."

"What do you do?"

"I'll tell you that on our tenth date."

"It's going to be difficult getting to the tenth date when there's not even going to be a first date." The dance was over and Carrie headed back to Peter as fast as she could.

"How did it go?" Peter asked.

"He's still a drip. In fact, he's a double drip, dancing with me and leaving his date sitting all alone."

"He doesn't have a date," Peter explained. "He said that he's just here until the intermission when he will make a few comments, and then he's out of here."

Sure enough, at intermission Mr. Worthington thanked everyone for their support of Samaritan Services, told a couple of heartwarming stories of how the charity had helped elderly residents of Sun View, and then asked the attendees to give more than just money. He explained how the charity could use volunteers. He was a very good speaker, very polished as if he had done this hundreds of times.

Now Carrie was curious. It seemed to be too late to find out any more about him. True to his word, he was out the door as soon as his little speech was over.

Oh, well, good riddance, Carrie thought.

I'll Hold You in My Heart 'Til I Can Hold You in My Arms

Peter called Carrie about once a week to see what was happening, so it was unusual for Carrie to hear from him twice in one day.

"I just had a very interesting call, Carrie."

"What's that?"

"Tom Worthington called and asked for your telephone number. He said that he had forgotten to get it."

"Did you give it to him?"

"No. I wouldn't do that without your permission."

"Good."

"I told him that I would have you call him."

"Oh, great. What for?"

"I'm sure he wants to ask you out."

"I can't call him."

"Why not? You should go out with him, Carrie. He seems like a really nice, classy guy."

"I'm sure he has some really basic flaw. He would be too good to be true otherwise."

"Oh, for pity sakes, Carrie, take a chance."

"That's all I've been doing for the last seven years. I'm tired of trying. No, I won't call him."

***

Two days later Peter called Carrie again. "Can you come over and help me? I have several wallpaper books here, and I need your decorating sense to tell me which paper to select."

"Okay, I'll be over shortly."

As Peter let her in the door, Carrie said, "It's a good thing you're such a great friend. I hate looking through wallpaper books."

"You'll survive. I've just got to do something with this kitchen. I don't want flowers or plaid or stripes or geometrics."

"Oh, great! All that's left is texture and the sponged look."

"That will be all right. I just have to find one I like." Just then the doorbell rang.

Carrie heard Peter say, "Tom. Come in. What a pleasant surprise!"

"Carrie, do you remember Tom Worthington?"

"Yes, of course. How are you, Mr. Worthington?"

"You can call me Tom if I may call you Carrie."

"It's a deal."

Tom, Peter, and Carrie had a pleasant conversation for about a half hour. Then Carrie said, "I've got to go and leave you two alone. I'll catch you tomorrow, Peter, and we can continue our wallpaper search."

Tom spoke up. "Oh, don't go. I just came to ask Peter a favor. Maybe you can help too, Carrie."

"What favor is that?"

"Well, I haven't dated much for the past several years, and there's this gal I would like to take out, but she doesn't seem interested. What should I do?"

"Why do you think she's not interested?" Carrie asked.

"She thinks I'm a boob. But the truth of the matter is, believe it or not, I don't have much experience with women. I got married quite young. When my wife died, I just didn't have any interest in dating, but now I'm really attracted to this gal. I fear I've lost all my chances by saying all the wrong things."

"Why don't you tell her what you've just told us?" Carrie suggested.

Peter and Tom smiled at each other as Tom said, "I just did. Will you go out with me, Carrie, and give me another chance?"

Carrie stuttered and stammered. "Well, yes, I guess so. Where and when?"

"Tomorrow night. Do you have Levis and cowboy boots?

"Levis but no boots."

"Great! Wear your Levis. I'll pick you up at seven.

***

"What the heck kind of a first date is that—Levis and cowboy boots?" Judy was not impressed.

"He doesn't know much about the dating world, so he says. Maybe he doesn't know he's supposed to wine and dine me and really try to impress me," Carrie said and laughed. "Maybe he knows I like country music and we're going to a concert. Maybe he's researched my interests."

Judy and Carrie looked at each, laughed, and said in unison, "No way."

***

Tom was right on time. "Have you figured out where we're going?"

"A concert?"

Tom said "No. Guess again." He was opening the car door for Carrie.

Omigod, Carrie thought, this is a very old Dodge Dart. So much for family money. This guy must have been the black sheep of the dynasty.

"No, we're going to a Country Western bar in Tampa."

Carrie's face lit up. "I love Country music. How did you know?"

Tom said, "I didn't know, but I'm glad to see I've finally scored some points with you."

"Yes, I've been listening to Country, especially Classic Country, for years. In fact, I'm trying to write a novel, and I'm entitling each chapter with the name of a favorite old Country music song."

"You don't seem like the type to like Country music—you're so sophisticated and all." Tom couldn't believe he was so lucky to find someone who shared his musical tastes.

"I think it's exactly because I do have a fairly complicated—you call it sophisticated, I call it complicated—life that I like Country. The music's so emotional and simple. Also, I've had many periods of loneliness in my life. I like the songs because there's solace in realizing that other people have suffered hurt and loneliness too. You know, misery loves company. That's the best way I can explain it. I've had other people be amazed about my love of Country, especially honky-tonk. How about you? You don't seem like a 'good ole country boy.'"

"I think you summed it up pretty well with your explanation." Tom didn't seem like he wanted to delve any deeper into his reasons. "By the way, please excuse my car. This is the car I use in my business."

"What business is that?"

"No, no. Remember I'm not telling until our tenth date."

Tom and Carrie danced the night away. They both were familiar with the Texas Two-Step but rusty in its execution. They had a lot of fun, though, and by the end of the evening were dancing like old pros.

***

"How was the date?" Peter was anxious to hear how his friends got along.

"We had a very nice time, but I smell the help of my good friend Peter in the whole evening."

"Why? What do you mean?"

"It seems awfully strange that he came over to your house when I was there and then took me to a Country Western bar, my favorite kind of evening out."

"I'll never tell. So how did the evening end, if you don't mind my asking?"

"He shook my hand."

"Man, I'm going to have to talk to him," Peter said.

"He's actually very much a gentleman. And he didn't say anything too weird all evening."

"Will you go out with him again?

"Probably. A poor guy who likes Country music is better than no one."

Just a Little Lovin' Will Go a Long Way

"I know I shouldn't be calling you the next day, but I had so much fun last night, I really would like to go out with you again…soon." It sounded to Carrie like Tom was in a bar. There was lots of background noise.

"Where are you?"

"I'm calling from work. I'm sorry about the noise, but there's not much private space here."

Carrie was happy to hear Tom's voice, but wanted to act cool even though she also had a good time. "Our going out again can probably be arranged."

"Okay, when?"

"How about Saturday night?"

"That sounds good. You were such a good sport going to a Country Western club so on this date I want to take you to an elegant restaurant."

"Oh, that's not necessary." Carrie was thinking of his 1968 Dodge Dart and how he might have trouble making ends meet.

"No, I insist. Put on your fanciest dress, and I'll pick you up at seven."

***

Carrie told Judy, "This should be interesting. What kind of place will this guy pick? If he does have a nice restaurant in mind, how weird will it be to pull up in an old car?"

"He surely has money. You said he admitted that his great grandfather had been very successful and earned a lot of money," Judy offered.

"I know but he says that he works and that he uses that old car for business. What kind of business could that be? I wish he would tell. I can't stand the suspense."

***

"Wow, what happened to the Dart?" Carrie couldn't help herself. She was shocked to see the car Tom had today—a late-model, fancy BMW. "This is a gorgeous car! Did you borrow it? I was happy in your Dart."

"No, this is my car too. The other one, as I mentioned to you, is for business, and because I have to loan it out a lot, I don't want anything too nice to use."

Tom and Carrie had a lovely evening. They had a candlelit dinner in a fine restaurant and talked for hours. The candlelight caused a beautiful glow on everything, the silver, the china, and on each of them. Somewhere along the line, Carrie brought up the subject of his wife's death. Although she could tell it was very painful for Tom, he told the story in a very factual way. They had wanted children for a long time. Finally, his wife got pregnant and carried the baby almost full-term. However, in the last month she contracted a virus which killed the fetus and then killed her. The baby had been a son. "Thomas Drake Worthington V," Tom added.

Carrie sincerely extended her condolences. She said, "Sometimes I feel sorry for myself for events in my life, but I have definitely never had anything that devastating happen to me."

"Tell me about some of the things for which you arc sorry," Tom said.

"Well, my first marriage ended in a divorce which I did not want. Then my second marriage was filled with my husband's sickness. He became ill three weeks after I married him and was sick for the entire marriage. He was a wonderful man, and I never minded taking care of him, but it was limiting. There were many things we could not do. Plus his care consumed a lot of my time. I really was lucky, though, because he never complained and was always thankful for everything I did for him."

They each talked a little longer of past painful experiences. Finally, Tom said, "That's enough pain for one evening. Let's dance. I liked this song that's piped in."

"There's no one dancing. I don't think we're supposed to dance here."

"There's hardly anyone left in this place. I'm sure they won't mind."

Carrie didn't object any more. She was anxious to be in Tom's arms. She was beginning to feel a great closeness to him. He didn't seem like such a bad guy after all.

Carrie and Tom danced to several songs, clinging to each other, without saying a word. Pretty soon, Tom lifted Carrie's face to his. Expecting a kiss on the lips, she was surprised to get a kiss on the forehead. "Thank you," Carrie murmured.

"Let's get out of here," Tom said abruptly and took her home.

***

"Damn, Carrie, at this rate, you'll be ninety before you get a proper kiss, let alone get to sleep with him. This certainly isn't a modern day romance where the couple ends up in bed on the first date." Judy was her usual feisty self.

"I guess he wants to take his time."

"That's the understatement of the year."

***

Carrie and Tom dated every two or three days for about three weeks. They dined out a lot, went to movies, attended concerts, and danced at their favorite Country Western bar. Their dates were always in the evening. Carrie asked Tom to come over during the day once but he begged off by saying,"No, I have to work."

Still no kisses. Carrie was getting concerned. She wondered if he didn't find her attractive. Finally she couldn't stand it any longer and said, "Tom, what's the problem? We have been dating for about a month. It seems like you like me. I can almost feel the chemistry when we dance, but you never kiss me on the lips, which I think would be appropriate after all this time. Aren't you attracted to me?"

"You've got to be kidding! I can hardly contain myself. I want to take you in my arms and kiss you for hours. You don't have to worry—I'm definitely all man. I didn't want to mess things up between us by getting physical too soon. And secondly, I want you to know my whole story before you become too involved with me."

"Speaking honestly, I think I've passed that point."

"Oh, boy, I guess it's time I shared an extremely important part of my life with you."

That night when he took Carrie home, he pulled her to him and kissed her fervently. Her knees were weak. She was lost in the scent of his after-shave lotion and in the strength of his arms wrapped around her. She had waited for this moment for so long, and she was not disappointed.

"I'll pick you up at eleven tomorrow morning. Be sure to wear Levis. I'm going to let you enter my "inner sanctum."

***

"What the heck could it be?" Carrie asked both Peter and Judy. "Where's he taking me? It must have something to do with his job as we're going during the day."

"You've definitely got me on this one," Judy ventured. "I have no earthly idea what's up."

"I sure hope it's not anything too strange or illegal or immoral. I really like this guy. In fact, I think I'm falling in love with him."

"You've definitely come a long way, baby," Peter added, reminding Carrie of her first encounters with Santa. Carrie laughed, too, as she thought of how much dislike she had had for Tom at first. It was a good thing he was persistent, she thought.

"I hope I can sleep tonight. This wondering is driving me crazy."

You Don't Know Me, The One Who Loves You So

Tom was right on time so Carrie assumed he stayed with his aunt on Platinum Drive, which was only a couple of miles from her, instead of at his home in Hyde Park. She had learned that he often stayed with his aunt to watch after her. She was quite elderly and really needed to be in an assisted living facility. She refused to go, though, so Tom looked after her a lot.

"Are you ready?"

"Ready!" Carrie was perky even though she had had very little sleep. She spent the night tossing, turning, and wondering where she was being taken by Tom. What does he do for a living? She could not put the pieces of the puzzle together.

Tom helped her into the Dart. "We're going in style again today," he kidded.

"Where are we going?" Carrie kept trying to solve the mystery.

"We're going to the warehouse district of Tampa. That's where I work."

"So you're in warehousing?"

"No. I needed a big place, away from the nice businesses, but close enough to downtown that my customers can walk to my building."

"Oh, for God's sake, Tom, what the heck do you do?"

"You'll see."

Somewhat irritated at being kept in the dark, Carrie stopped asking questions, and they just rode in silence through Tampa. *What the hell is all the secrecy? You'd think he's an FBI agent or in the CIA.*

After about a twenty minute ride, Tom pulled into the parking lot of an old warehouse that did have a fresh coat of paint. "This is it."

They walked around the front of the building. There, on the front, was a sign that said "Light and Life Mission." Omigod, Carrie thought, he's a minister. No wonder he took so long to kiss me. I hope he's not a priest going over the wall. Carrie's thoughts were running wild.

"You work in a mission?"

"I founded this mission, and yes, I do work here everyday. It's lunch time. Are you going to help me with the food line? We're always short-handed."

"Well...sure...yes, I will. Just show me what to do."

The "customers," as Tom called them, started filing in. Tom knew most of them by name and introduced every one to Carrie. "Carrie's our new soup lady," he would say to them. There was Maria, Joseph, Twitch, Jose, Beerbelly, and many more whose names Carrie couldn't remember. The names just kept rolling out of Tom's mouth.

Lunch lasted about two hours, and then the cleanup started. Carried found herself cleaning and drying lots of big kettles. After a while, she collapsed in one of the dining room chairs.

"Oh, no, you don't. We have to check the beds." Tom was enjoying showing Carrie how hard he worked.

"Do you need a hand, Felicia?"

"I can always use a hand, Mr. Tom, these beds don't change themselves."

"We have to change the beds everyday and wash the bedding. There are no assigned beds so no telling who will sleep in a bed at night. Felicia spends most of her day getting the beds set up. She's one of the few paid staff members."

Tom showed Carrie around the mission. Besides the kitchen, dining room, and dormitory, there was a laundry room, a living room area, and a chapel, which was quite pretty.

As Tom showed Carrie a big meeting room, Carrie spoke up, "Why do you have a meeting room? I can't imagine that too many meetings go on here."

"To the contrary, we have a lot of meetings. We have AA meetings and what we call 'classes' but I'll be telling you all about that later. Let's get out of here now. I'll make it a short day today in your honor."

Carrie and Tom drove a few blocks in silence. Then all of a sudden, Carrie said, "Wow, Tom, so this is what you do, day in and day out?"

"Yes, it is. It's my life's work."

"You don't work in your family's business at all?"

"No, my brother takes care of everything. It's mostly managing portfolios now. Granddaddy's business was sold several years ago."

Instead of going back to Sun View, Tom headed for St. Petersburg. He wanted to show Carrie the Don Cezar Hotel and Restaurant at sunset. She had been there before but never with anyone she cared about. He took her hand and led her over the little wooden bridge that led to the beach. They sat in the wooden chairs there and watched the beautiful sunset. "It's like this almost every day. I come here often, always alone, though."

"This is incredibly beautiful," she said.

"I need to see beauty every once in while after seeing so much pain and suffering all day long," Tom said.

"Carrie, I want to talk to you. Please, just listen to me for a few minutes before saying anything. I think you know that I'm falling in love with you. And I think you feel the same way. Am I right?"

Carrie's stomach turned over. She was glad she was sitting down. She was amazed at Tom's forthrightness. All she could muster was, "Yes, I do feel the same way." She couldn't even manage the word "love."

"Good. However, Carrie, I don't want to go any further in this relationship unless you accept what I do and will help me with it. But I can understand how you wouldn't want to. Anyone in his or her right mind would not want to get involved in mission work. It's rough. It's sad. It's grueling. There are not a lot of happy endings."

Carrie started to answer, but Tom waved her off. "I'm not done. I don't want your answer now. You don't know enough about my work yet. If you think you might be interested, I want you to work side by side with me for a week. Then I want you to take a week off and not see me at all. I want you to think about my life and whether or not you want to share it. After the second week, we'll go away for three days and discuss our future, or lack thereof. How does that sound?"

Carrie was stunned and speechless. For starters, she didn't realize that Tom was falling in love with her so his words were a shocker. She was thrilled but astonished. She thought Tom would be the sort who would wait several years, or at least several months, before he admitted his deepest feelings. For all of his sophistication, he was quite unsophisticated when it came to expressing emotions. This was truly amazing. Then to be faced with a life very different than what she had envisioned for herself was startling also. "It sounds like a plan," was all she could say.

After a short walk on the beach and dinner in the outdoor, ocean-side restaurant, Tom drove Carrie home. At her door, he swept her into his arms and gave her another wonderful kiss. In fact, he couldn't stop kissing her. They stood there for several minutes loving each other. He started to kiss her neck, and she could feel his heavy breathing. "I've got to go," he said abruptly. "I'll pick you up at eight tomorrow morning."

"Eight a.m.?"

"Mission work has early and long hours."

As soon as Tom was out of sight, Carrie jumped in her car and headed to Judy's. Even if she did have to get up early, she needed to talk with Judy. "Judy, Judy, Judy, I need to talk with you," Carrie said, using the expression that Judy had heard a million times.

"What's happening? Don't tell me you're in love again. I wish I had a dollar for every time you've told me this same story."

"This time is different," Carrie said with a pleading look in her eye. "It really is."

"Yeah, right," Judy said.

"No, really. He's everything I ever wanted in a man, and he says he loves me."

"What's so different about that?" Judy wasn't convinced.

"I'm not sure, but there's something different. Maybe it's because he's a sincerely nice guy, not flamboyant at all, not my usual type. He's very caring, not just about me, but about every one and every thing. He's just a lovely guy whom I don't deserve. Besides, he's got a job, doesn't have kids, and doesn't have an ex-wife hanging around. Why wouldn't every gal in the world fall in love with this guy?"

Judy was ready to let Carrie have it. "First of all, this guy doesn't have a job; he's got a mission that he gives his all to. You're not going to like that. You want to have fun. You want jewelry, vacations, and a social lifestyle. His lifestyle is giving to others. That's what he does for a job and what he does for kicks. It's his whole life."

"You're right, Judy, in everything you say. But maybe I've changed just a little. In watching Tom in action, I see I've missed something big in life—giving to others. Oh, I do a little volunteer work in Sun View, but it isn't really very much and certainly doesn't put me out any. His type of work seems very rewarding and all consuming. I'll soon find out because I'm going to work for a week with Tom in the mission. When I watch Tom counseling others and helping them get on the right foot, jewelry and vacations seem sort of frivolous."

Judy continued, "Secondly, if Tom is such a wonderful person with very little baggage, how are you going to explain away your life?"

"What do you mean?"

"Well, your life has not exactly been filled with good deeds. How are you going to explain away all of your lovers? Your many nights spent drinking in smoky bars? Nights filled with pot and orgies? Shall I go on?"

"No, I get your point. I'm just not going to tell him," Carrie explained.

"Carrie, it's going to come out. You'll meet someone from your past who will need to be explained. Or, if nothing else, you will get tired of keeping your past secret or you'll start to feel repressed. You'll have one too many glasses of wine one night, and it will all come spilling out."

"Okay, I will tell him all about my past before we get too involved."

"Hold the phone! I don't think that's a good idea. If you do anything, you need to just suggest that you have some skeletons in your closet. See what he says. If he wants details, tell him some of the less racy stories. That should satisfy him."

After thinking about what Judy said for a few moments, Carrie said, "Okay. But I feel I should make a clean sweep of everything."

"Carrie, get real. If you make a clean sweep of everything, you'll have a great big pile of rubble that even the most forgiving guy might have trouble getting around."

"Okay, Judy, I'll take your advice. And have I ever told you that I love you. You're the greatest friend. Putting up with all my shit and never judging me. You're the greatest." Carrie was crying now and hugging her friend.

Searching for Someone Like You

"By the time we get there this morning, breakfast will be over. I have an early morning crew that takes care of that. Everyone has to be out of bed by six-thirty a.m. and has to have his or her morning meal over by eight a.m." Tom had picked up Carrie right on time. She was ready and anxious to start working with Tom in the mission. She listened intently as he explained the morning routine.

"So we won't have anything to do until lunch?"

"I don't want to laugh at you, but that really is pretty funny. You'll see that there is never a second to sit down and rest," Tom gently explained.

Tom and Carrie arrived at the mission just as the morning service in the chapel was starting. "The customers are not required to attend but we really encourage them to. They need to have a spiritual element to their lives. For some of them that's pretty much all they have—knowing that God loves them. They need to be reminded of that frequently."

Carrie gazed all around at the chapel. It was really quite beautiful, she thought, far prettier than she would have imagined in a warehouse mission. The ceiling had arched timbers, forming a peak the length of the chapel. The pews were wooden too, probably out of some old country church. The highlight of the chapel was a large stained glass window at the front, behind the altar. It was a very colorful picture of Jesus with both of his arms outstretched, like he was inviting someone to come into his fold.

"Who's the minister?" Carrie asked.

"He's a friend of mine, Reverend Nigel, who stops by every morning, and I thank God for him. He was asked to leave his regular church for some improprieties. I've never asked for details. All I know is that he is wonderful with our people. About once a month he gives a talk on forgiveness, and it is powerful. I imagine he is speaking from experience."

"Are you religious, Tom?"

"Well, yes, I guess I am. I definitely believe in God. How about you, Carrie?"

"Yes, I also believe in God. I don't understand how anyone cannot believe. If you look all around this world, at the human system, the plant systems, the animal systems, and so forth, I just don't understand how anyone could think that it all happened by accident. The planning and design are exquisite—definitely planned by a supreme being."

"Wow, that's exactly how I feel! We'll have to talk about that some more. The service is starting now, and I want you to see and hear it all."

The service was a half-hour long and pretty much like any church service. The one difference was that Carrie saw several of the men crying. Crying over misspent lives, she assumed. In fact, Carrie was so moved that she began crying, softly but obvious to Tom.

After the service, Tom asked about the tears.

Carrie tried to explain. "I usually cry when I go to church. Mother, while she was alive, never wanted to sit with me because of it. The only thing I can think of is that I cry because I'm ashamed of the life I've lived."

"You know Jesus died for our sins. God forgives. Besides, I doubt that your life has been that bad."

Carrie sure didn't want to tell Tom of her past life. Fortunately, Tom didn't seem too concerned. He said, "Let's go down to Meeting Room A now. I conduct a half-hour AA meeting there every morning."

"Are a lot of these guys and gals alcoholics?" Carrie assumed they were but wanted to hear the details from Tom.

"Yes, a lot of them have alcohol problems. Or have had in the past. We don't want them falling off the wagon again."

Just then Twitch came up to Tom. "I think you had better talk with Joe. I think he's drinking again."

"Okay, try to get him in here, and I will talk with him after the meeting. He's working night shift now, right?"

Carrie watched Tom conduct the meeting and wondered if she would ever have to run it. Tom started by asking if anyone had anything to celebrate. Most of the ten or so guys all told how long they had been sober. Some had been sober for a couple of years, but for most, it was more like a couple of months, and for some, it was days. The group congratulated everyone no matter how long it had been.

Tom reviewed what they should do if they felt like having a drink. Each one had a mentor, usually a recovering alcoholic himself. They were to get in touch with that person and talk about their desires. If they couldn't reach their mentor, they were to come to the mission and talk with Tom or Carrie.

Carrie! Carrie sat upright. Had she heard right? She was going to have to counsel alcoholics already? Tom introduced Carrie to the guys. They all applauded.

Afterwards Carrie said to Tom, "I am glad that you have confidence in me that I could counsel, but I don't really feel qualified. What do I say?"

"I'm going to get you some training. In the meantime, what you do mostly is listen. You try to find out what they feel most frustrated about and help them develop a plan to overcome the frustration, whatever it is."

"Come with me while I speak with Joe as Twitch asked me to do." Tom took Carrie's hand and led her to another meeting room, the one where he counseled one-on-one.

"Hi, Joe, how's it going?"

"Okay." Joe seemed very sad.

"Twitch said that he was worried that you might have started drinking again. You're not, are you, Joe?"

"Well, I had a couple of drinks, but I'm not back to my drinking ways of the old days."

"Joe, what's the matter? You know it's dangerous for a recovering alcoholic to have even one drink, right? What's going on? We got you a job. Don't you like it?"

"No, I love my job. I guess I just worry that I'll screw up and lose this job too. Drinking eases my worries."

"Joe, you can't think that way. You should just do your job everyday the best that you can do. Yes, you might lose your job. Lots of people are losing their jobs. Just don't make drinking the reason. If you do your job well and don't drink, even if you lose your job, we can probably help you get another one. Stop worrying so much and just enjoy your job. Okay? And I want to see you in the AA meeting every day for a couple of weeks."

Afterwards, Carrie asked, "Is getting the guys jobs part of this mission?"

"Oh yes, a very big part. Let's go start working on lunch, Carrie."

By the end of the day, Carrie felt like her brain was swirling with all the information, procedures, and stories she had heard. She felt like going home and soaking for a long time in a warm bath. However, as soon as Tom suggested dinner at Don Cesar, she perked up.

They repeated the evening of a couple of days ago. He led her once again to the chairs by the water. She took her shoes off. The cool sand felt so good between her toes and under her tired feet.

"How did you ever get into mission work, Tom?"

"You really want to hear that story, Carrie?"

"Yeah, I do. I just can't imagine a man who has everything wanting to give most of it up to help the downtrodden. Don't get me wrong. I think it's wonderful, but how did it all start?"

"My life turned upside down when my wife and son died. I didn't want to do anything. I certainly didn't want to manage my family's business, which is what I was doing. It all seemed so pointless."

"You must have been severely depressed," Carrie offered.

"No, I don't think I was depressed. Sad, yes, but not depressed. I certainly wasn't suicidal, and I knew that I would be able to pick up the pieces of my life and go on. However, my work seemed meaningless. Who was I helping other than myself? I started thinking that I had been put on earth for bigger things."

"Gee, you were helping all the people who worked in your companies. They probably needed their jobs."

"Yes, that's true, and I did feel bad selling the companies. I did make sure that no one got laid off in the transition, and I gave each one a nice bonus paycheck. However, I just knew that I had to do more."

Carrie was still puzzled about why he settled on mission work. "There are lots of ways that you can do good in this life. Why did you decide to build a mission?"

"About the time that I was floundering about, I met George Nigel, you know, the pastor you met. He was pretty down and out himself. He was associating with a lot of street people through a temporary job he took. He starting telling me how there was really a need for someplace for the homeless to go for a good meal. There were some facilities around for them but not enough and not ones that tried to rehabilitate them. That's when I got the idea to start a mission, and the rest is history, as they say."

"And you just started a mission? Just like that?"

"Well, there was a lot to it, but I threw myself into the project and have never looked back. Haven't you heard enough of this for one night."

"I guess so. Are you ready to take me home."

"Can you handle another day at Light and Life tomorrow?"

"Definitely. I find the work fascinating. Tiring but fascinating."

On the way home, Carrie just had to ask. She couldn't stand it any longer. "Why have you never taken me to your home in Hyde Park? I've had you over to my house."

"Well, in case you don't realize it, I was taken with you the first time I danced with you at the Samaritan Ball. You know, when you thought I was a complete fool, or worse."

"Go on."

"I just decided then and there that, if I ever had a second chance with you, I would keep my family's money from you until you liked me for me. If you were to see my house, you would see that it is quite grand. You might get the wrong idea about me too soon."

"Well, I did wonder what was going on. First you admitted that your great grandfather had been very ambitious and successful. Then you show up in an old car. Then the next time you show up in a nice new car. You definitely had me guessing."

Tom continued, "Don't get me wrong. I'm very appreciative of the fact that I don't have to struggle to make ends meet. But really, money means very little to me at this point. I would move into a room at the mission if I had to and be quite happy as long as I felt I was helping someone. Say good night, Carrie."

Carrie jumped out of the car, and, acting as lighthearted as she felt, said, "Good night, Carrie." Tom was waiting while she let herself in the door. Then all of a sudden, she ran back to the car and gave Tom a great big kiss.

"That's very nice, Sweetheart. I'll pick you up at eight a.m. tomorrow."

***

Tom and Carrie worked side by side all week long. There wasn't a job in the mission that Carrie didn't help with. She even tried counseling a couple of the gals that came into the mission for the first time. Carrie assessed their needs to see how they might help them. Tom was very pleased with her work.

By the time Friday night arrived, Carrie was tired but exhilarated. She enjoyed the work at the mission. And she loved working with Tom. He was such a kind man to everyone. She was very impressed with his devotion to the mission and the "customers". Tom didn't like to call them patients or visitors or guests, certainly not inmates.

Tom said at about five in the evening, "Will you go with me to Don Cesar one more time?"

"Only one more time?" Carrie asked.

"Well, what I mean is that next week I won't see you and we won't be spending any evenings watching the sunsets," Tom explained. "You know, if you go along with my plan, next week you'll spend reflecting on this past week at the mission and deciding if it's a life for you."

"Oh, I haven't forgotten. I'm ready to think about it, but I really think I already...."

At that point, Tom interrupted. "No, don't go on. I want you to take the week and really think how different life will be for you and what you'll be giving up if you take up this crazy life with me."

"And don't forget, I'll be thinking of what I'll be gaining too," Carrie said with eyes twinkling.

"Please, Carrie, take my request seriously. I'm thinking of myself too. I don't want to feel that I got you into something you hate. I would feel guilty the rest of my life."

"Well, while we're having a heart-to-heart talk, I want to discuss something with you. I also would feel guilty the rest of my life if you learn more about me and are disappointed. I haven't exactly told you about my past life. In fact, we have been so wrapped in the day-to-day operation of the mission, we really haven't discussed my past at all.

"I don't really care about your past," Tom said. "What I care about is now and our future together."

"My life has not been very Christian-like," Carrie said.

"Whose has been?" Tom challenged.

"No, I mean I have done a lot of things I'm really ashamed of and wish I hadn't done."

"I don't care."

"But what if it comes out some way in the future."

"Look, Carrie, I'll deal with it then. I've heard so many stories in my day-to-day work. I'm shock-proof. Besides I know you as a very loving, giving person now. What's past is past. I can't change it. Maybe your past caused you to be the wonderful person you are today. Have you ever thought about that? Let's forget your past. If something rears its ugly head in the future, I promise not to be shocked and not to leave you, okay."

Tom and Carrie held hands while they watched the sun go down then they headed home. As Tom said goodbye to Carrie and prepared to be apart from her for a week, he said, "Good-bye, Carrie. Just remember I love you, the person you are today. Forget the past." After a very clinging, passionate good-night kiss, Tom and Carrie went their separate ways.

Behind Closed Doors

Carrie spent the week alone as Tom had asked her to do. At first she was so tired from working very hard at the mission the past week that she didn't mind. By the time she was thoroughly rested, though, she was lonely—profoundly lonely. She missed Tom so much. She actually missed the mission and all the activity there, too.

"Whatcha doing?" Judy asked as she let herself in the back door to Carrie's house.

"I'm reviewing my jewelry."

"What on earth for?"

"I'm thinking of each piece, who gave it to me, and under what circumstances the gift was given. There are lots of memories wrapped up in this jewelry. However, I think it's time for me to dole it out to all my eighteen nieces and nieces-in-law. I don't need all of it anymore. I'll keep a few special pieces, but I want to give the rest away to relatives. That's what I have specified in my will. I might as well do it now."

"Wait, a minute. Hold the phone. Let me understand—the woman whose big goal in life was to find a man who would shower her with gifts is now going to give the gifts away?" Judy couldn't believe what she was hearing.

"I think so. For some reason, they just don't mean that much to me anymore."

"I think Tom and his crazy life have gotten to you," Judy said.

"It's not a crazy life; it's a wonderful life. I know I can't believe I'm saying this either. I've got all week to make up my mind about what I want to do, but I feel like I'm ready to let him know my decision."

"You had better really analyze this before jumping out of a very comfortable lifestyle. You worked hard all your life to earn your golden years. Now you want to go to work everyday at eight a.m.? I don't think so."

"I love Tom. There's no doubt in mind about that. But more than that, I actually love the mission work."

"You just love working side by side with Tom," Judy corrected Carrie.

"No, you're wrong. There's something wonderful in feeling like you're helping others. I never helped anyone in my life other than myself. I never had children so I never felt nurturing or maternal. Maybe the mission is an outlet for all those feelings."

"Could be. You did take care of two husbands, though. Doesn't that count?"

"For some reason, in my mind it doesn't. Besides, Tom says that our life won't all be filled with selfless activities. He says he likes to take nice vacations. Also, he has a house in Hyde Park, which I have never seen, but there are no slums in Hyde Park, to say the least."

"I wonder why he's never taken you there."

"There's never been a reason to. Remember, we haven't spent the night together."

"Oh, yes, when are you going to check out that aspect of your relationship? You don't want to buy a pig in a poke, so to speak. Don't you want to make sure that you won't have to spend the rest of your life without sex?"

"I can just tell that we won't have a problem in that department," Carrie said as she smiled and winked at Judy.

"Are you sure you're in love with Tom? I mean, after all, you've been in love with dozens of men."

"Well, think about it. He's a wonderful person, very caring, loving, and fun. He has no addictions, no children to cause problems, no money problems, and he loves me. I should be shouting from the housetops! What's not to love?"

Carrie went on, "I'm tired of living out the lyrics of Country Western songs. I'm tired of listening to 'he done me wrong' songs. Please, Dear God, let me have a love story with a happy ending."

"So you're going to say 'yes' to Tom?"

"I'm going to say 'yes' to anything he proposes, and that's that!"

***

"God, did I miss you!" Tom called on Sunday evening just as he promised he would.

"Yeah, me too. I even missed the mission."

"Do you really mean that?"

"With all my heart."

"I'm afraid to ask the question. In fact, I'm not going to ask it yet. Will you go away with me for a few days and we can spend the time talking about what's going to happen next."

"Just talking?" joked Carrie.

"Well, maybe not all talking."

***

It was just a two hour trip to Bonita Springs, but it passed quickly as Tom caught Carrie up on all the activities at the mission. Tom had made reservations at the Hyatt's Coconut Plantation, a timeshare unit he owned. There weren't too many people there as the resort had been open only six months.

Each unit was an apartment, decorated in the style of a plantation. In fact, the decorations were beautiful. Carrie couldn't believe they would put this expensive furniture in a time-share unit. The tables were all beautiful dark wood with a lot of engraving and detail work. A lot of the sofas and chairs were luxurious leather. As Tom showed Carrie through the rooms, he stopped at the bedroom.

"Look at that bed—it's very high."

"Yes, I guess that's the plantation style too," Carrie offered.

Tom took Carrie in his arms and said, "Look, there are only one bedroom and one bed in this place. Are you okay with that, Carrie? I could sleep on the sofa."

Carrie gave Tom a tender kiss on the cheek. "Yes, I'm okay. You don't have to sleep in the living room. Want to try the bed out now?"

Tom tried not to act surprised. In his mind, he cancelled sipping wine on the balcony and watching a beautiful sunset. Best not to keep a lady waiting, he thought.

Carrie went to the bathroom and changed into a silk negligee. When she came out, Tom was nowhere around so she just slipped into bed. When he returned, he had several lit candles on a tray that lent a beautiful glow to the room.

As he started to take his clothes off, Carrie turned her back to him so as to not see him undress. He slipped into bed and immediately nestled up to her back. She could tell that his lean and trim body was totally naked. He rubbed her back and started giving her neck light kisses. He rubbed her back for several minutes.

"Omigosh, that feels so good."

"I'm going to make you feel really good."

"What are you going to do to me?"

"You'll see," Tom said as he gently turned Carrie over. The movement caused her breast to fall out of her gown. Tom took advantage of the situation by kissing her nipple. A low moan from Carrie made Tom realize that she was not unhappy. Not wanting to rush anything, Tom immediately switched to rubbing her feet and lower legs. Carrie kept moaning her approval.

"I'm not doing anything for you," Carrie whispered.

"You will, darling. You will," Tom said as his hand rubbed higher and higher on her thighs. In one swift move, he pulled her nightgown all the way up to her waist and started kissing and licking her belly.

"This is wonderful, Tom. You are quite the lover."

"I want you to be really ready for lovemaking. Okay?"

Carrie could hardly control herself to ease out the answer, "Okay."

Suddenly, Tom moved his finger to her epicenter. As he massaged, Carrie was literally shaking all over and moaning. After a few minutes, her moaning got low and guttural. At that moment, Tom got on top of her and penetrated her. She was definitely ready and so was he. As he thrust inside her, she was saying, almost as a chant, "Don't ever leave me. I love you. I love this. I've got to have this all the time." Her conversation drove Tom wild, and he climaxed almost immediately.

"Oh...my...God...was that great! I'm sorry I came so quickly," Tom apologized.

"There'll be other times when we can practice coming at the same time."

"Did you have an orgasm, Carrie?"

"Yes, several. Couldn't you tell?"

"No, I really couldn't, but I'm glad for you. Did you mean what you said while in the throes of lovemaking?"

"About loving you? Yes, with every ounce of my being."

Tom and Carrie kissed with all the fervor of two lovers whose energy had not yet been spent. However, after the kiss, they both fell into a deep, relaxing sleep in each other's arms.

I Will Always Love You

Sure enough, in the next few days, Tom and Carrie perfected their lovemaking. They were definitely enjoying the physical relationship. For all the lovey-dovey stuff, though, they made time to talk about the future.

"Asking you questions about our future still makes me nervous. I guess I'm afraid the answer is not going to be the one I want to hear, but I'm going to ask anyway," Tom said. "You say you love me, but is it a strong enough love to share my life in the mission?"

"Yes, Tom, I'm sure it is," Carrie said with all the conviction she could garner. She wanted to make sure there was no mistaking her intentions.

"You know it's a lot of hard work."

"Yes, you demonstrated that to me many times the week before last. I think I have a good feel for the work and know I can be a big help to you."

"Wonderful!" As he said this, he put his arms around Carrie and drew her close.

"In fact, I'm convinced you could use some of my skills."

"Which skills are those?" Tom was curious now and drew back.

"You need, for instance, my fundraising talents."

"I didn't know you worked in fundraising."

"I didn't. But, as you know, I worked for years in marketing and sales at Xerox. Fundraising is just a variation of marketing and sales."

"Wow, you're right, that would be great! I'm not too interested in that part of the job, but I know it's important. In fact, paramount." Tom was excited now about getting help in new areas.

"See, I have been thinking about the mission and how I can help. Like last week I spent a lot of time analyzing my feelings. Once I realized I wanted to spend my life with you in mission work, I switched to figuring out how I could be most useful."

Tom was surprised by this and took her hand. "Then, I have an important question for you Carrie."

"What's that?" There was a big smile on her face. She really thought she had figured out both the question and the answer.

Tom dropped to his knees and held both of Carrie's hands. "Will you make me the happiest man on earth and accept my proposal of marriage?"

Tom was surprised as she pulled her hands away to cover her face. He realized she was crying. "What's wrong, Sweetheart?"

"Nothing's wrong. Everything's right." Carrie wiped away her tears, and shouted, "Yes! Yes! I will marry you. I'm just overcome with emotion. Having been lonely for so long, I just can't believe I can be this deliriously happy."

***

Tom and Carrie returned to working at the mission after their short vacation. Everyone was glad to have them back and accepted Carrie as though she had always been a member of the team. True to her word, in addition to helping in the kitchen and food lines at lunch and dinner, she spent the in-between hours working on fundraising. She also realized that she could be useful by applying for grants, another area Tom did not work in too often.

One day, out of the blue, he said, "When can I make an honest woman of you? When do you want to get married?" Tom and Carrie had been living together at his beautiful old Hyde Park home ever since their trip together.

Carrie was so happy with their life she had basically forgotten the detail of a wedding. "I've got an idea. Why don't we just get married in the chapel here? It's lovely, and we can have all the mission people come share our day with us. That seems only appropriate."

"Oh, no. For the most important day of our lives, I want to share it with all of our friends and family. I want you to have a beautiful church wedding. Didn't you say you have a cousin living in Hyde Park whose husband is the pastor at a Christian church there? Let's get married in their church."

"Are you sure you want to go all out for this ceremony?"

"Absolutely!"

Carrie realized she was not going to change Tom's mind, and secretly she had always dreamed of a beautiful wedding too.

***

Carrie waited in the back of the old church, silhouetted by the beautiful stained glass windows and happy she had chosen this time of day to get married. The setting sun produced a glow in the windows, yet it was dark enough in the church to have candlelight. Partial to a soft glow for all romantic occasions, Tom had made sure there were candles everywhere.

Carrie was so glad Tom had insisted on a church wedding, not one in the chapel. She loved her beautiful flowing ivory gown, the roses in her bouquet, and all the roses intermingled with the candles at the end of each pew. There were so many candles at the altar in standing candelabras that the front of the church radiated such beauty that Carrie was awestruck

The wedding march began, and Carrie started down the aisle. Carrie was behind her only attendant Judy. As she slowly passed the pews, she saw many of her friends and family. There was Peter sitting next to his latest girlfriend and beaming from ear to ear. He was truly happy for Carrie and Tom and felt good about being instrumental in getting them together during those first few, almost-ill-fated days.

There was Alan Johnson, beaming at Judy with love in his eyes. It looked like Judy had made a love connection too.

As the bride approached the altar, she saw Tom watching her with all the love in the world filling his eyes. Her throat tightened when she suddenly noticed her friends from the mission, dressed in all the finery they could muster for the occasion—at least fifty of the town's poorest street people—filling the front pews. They seemed excited and craned their heads to see Carrie as she passed. She was overwhelmed. It was just like Tom to make sure all of them were invited, probably bused them in, and had them occupy the best seats in the church.

Carrie's eyes welled up in tears as she took his hand. She knew that with such a dedicated, loving man as Tom by her side, her life was truly going to have a happy ending—no more sad Country songs for her!